A Tale Rooted in Reality

Silent Promises: Dreams Over Love

"When love and ambition collide, only one can be the victor"

ANUBHAV SINGH

NewDelhi • London

BLUEROSE PUBLISHERS
India | U.K.

Copyright © Anubhav Singh Gangwar 2024

All rights reserved by author. No part of this publication may be reproduced, stored in a retrieval system or transmitted in any form or by any means, electronic, mechanical, photocopying, recording or otherwise, without the prior permission of the author. Although every precaution has been taken to verify the accuracy of the information contained herein, the publisher assumes no responsibility for any errors or omissions. No liability is assumed for damages that may result from the use of information contained within.

BlueRose Publishers takes no responsibility for any damages, losses, or liabilities that may arise from the use or misuse of the information, products, or services provided in this publication.

For permissions requests or inquiries regarding this publication, please contact:

BLUEROSE PUBLISHERS
www.BlueRoseONE.com
info@bluerosepublishers.com
+91 8882 898 898
+4407342408967

ISBN: 978-93-6783-815-0

Cover design: Daksh
Typesetting: Tanya Raj Upadhyay

First Edition: November 2024

Table of Contents

Part 1: The Beginning 1
   Chapter 1: Small Town Dreams 2
   Chapter 2: City Encounter 11

Part 2: Scenes 21
   Chapter 3: Terms of Agreement 22
   Chapter 4: A Leap of Faith 44
   Chapter 5: Clashing Worlds 53

Part 3: Perspective Shifts 70
   Chapter 6: Unwritten Emotions 71
   Chapter 7: Breaking Boundaries 105

Part 4: The Crossroads of Destiny 118
   Chapter 8: A Serene Private Space 119
   Chapter 9: A New Understanding 132
   Chapter 10: Silent Departures 148

Part 1:
The Beginning

Chapter 1: Small Town Dreams

"Introduce the protagonist, a 22-year-old boy from a modest middle-class family in a small town. Explore his aspirations, struggles, and the societal expectations that shape his life. He dreams of making it big in the city but feels confined by his circumstances"

Aarav sat on the edge of his bed, the weight of the world resting on his shoulders. The dim light of dawn filtered through the thin curtains of his small room in Bareilly, illuminating posters of airplanes and cityscapes plastered on the walls—silent testaments to his dreams. At 22, he was the youngest in his family, a quiet boy with aspirations that soared far above the confines of his modest upbringing.

Born into a middle-class family, Aarav's life was shaped by both his dreams and the societal expectations that surrounded him. His parents, though loving, were practical. His father worked as a Lawyer in a local court, while his mother managed the household, meticulously budgeting their limited resources. They had sacrificed so much to ensure that Aarav and his siblings had access to education, but the sacrifices often came with an unspoken weight of responsibility.

Aarav's journey began in the local government school, where he often found himself lost in the pages of adventure novels rather than focusing on his studies. His grades reflected this distraction—average marks that didn't inspire much confidence from his teachers or family. The pressure to perform weighed heavily on him, especially compared to his older siblings, who had excelled in their studies and paved promising paths. His siblings had bright futures ahead; Aarav often felt like he was trailing behind.

Aarav's journey after high school was anything but easy. Scoring poorly in both his 10th and 12th exams, he was left grappling with the shattered dream of becoming a doctor. The weight of his family's financial burdens pressed down on him, and with no other options, he enrolled in a government college for a Bachelor of Business Administration. The college wasn't glamorous, but for Aarav, it was a flicker of hope, a stepping stone to something better.

However, the struggles were far from over. Aarav had completed his schooling in Hindi medium, but now everything—from lectures to exams—was in English. Each day felt like a battle, not just against the coursework but against the deep-seated fear that maybe he wasn't enough and to add to his load, he took on part-time jobs to support his own expenses, all while preparing for the MBA entrance exams. Nights stretched into early mornings as he juggled responsibilities, his dreams of a different life flickering in the back of his mind, pushing him to keep going.

Despite the hurdles life had thrown his way, Aarav finally graduated, clutching his degree like a lifeline to a brighter future. But deep down, he knew that his struggles were far from over. The job market was fierce, and without an MBA, his chances of distinguishing himself seemed bleak. The path to his dreams was steep, but he was determined. He applied for the CAT exam and scored well, but that victory only opened the door to more challenges—money being the biggest.

Aarav had set his sights on some of the best business schools in India, but the reality of his financial situation made those options seem distant. After trying for various prestigious universities, the only viable option was a newly established university in Punjab. While he was fortunate enough to secure a scholarship, it barely covered his tuition fees, leaving the looming costs of personal expenses and accommodation to be managed. Aarav's heart felt heavy as he signed the loan papers, aware that this decision placed an additional burden on his already struggling family.

And then, the day arrived. The acceptance letter came like a long-awaited breath of fresh air, but the victory felt bittersweet. There was no grand celebration—just Aarav, sitting alone with the letter in his hands, feeling the weight of his family's dreams pressing down on him. It was a personal triumph, but one tinged with quiet anxiety.

When Aarav finally arrived at the university in Punjab, it was as if he had stepped into a dream. The infrastructure was far more impressive than he had imagined, and the campus buzzed with students from every corner of India and even abroad. Despite the excitement, Aarav felt a wave of tension wash over him. This new, crowded world seemed overwhelming, and he questioned how he would carve out a place for himself here.

But he refused to give in to doubt. Late into the nights, while the world around him slept, Aarav sat under dim lights, poring over textbooks, his determination unwavering. Coffee became his closest ally as he studied relentlessly, trying to stay ahead in a language and environment that felt foreign. All the while, the suffocating pressure of financial strain wrapped itself tighter around him, but he persevered, driven by the silent promise he had made to himself and his family.

Despite of his effort, Aarav's performance in the first two semesters in MBA was disheartening. He struggled to keep his scholarship alive, watching his dream slip further from his grasp. But when he realized there was no other option, something in him shifted.

He buckled down, using every spare moment—even during his summer internship—to study for the upcoming semesters. His hard work paid off, and by the third and fourth semesters, he ranked among the top students. It was a triumph, but his journey didn't end there.

Despite the steady climb in his grades, campus placements remained elusive for Aarav. The hopes he'd carefully built through hard work and persistence began to feel flimsy, like a house of cards swaying in the wind. Yet, giving up was never an option. He returned to his hometown, Bareilly, a place that pulsed with memories, far removed from the bustling campuses and busy corridors where he'd chased his dreams.

The city greeted him with a sense of familiarity that was both comforting and sobering. Its quieter streets were worlds apart from the ambitious whirlpool he'd left behind. Undeterred, Aarav dived into the job search with fervor. Day after day, he scoured job listings, sent out applications, and reached out to companies, each effort underscored by the fear of rejection but the determination to break through. For two relentless months, he endured the waiting and uncertainty, until one day, his efforts bore fruit. He secured a position with an international airline.

It wasn't the position he'd once dreamed of, but it was a start—a foothold in the future he'd sacrificed so much for. The day he departed for his new job felt monumental. As Aarav stepped off the train into the city that now held his future, he was engulfed by a surge of excitement tempered by trepidation. The clamor of honking horns, the sea of strangers bustling past him—all the chaotic energy of the place hit him at once, awakening both anxiety and hope. He paused, taking it all in, steadying himself for the journey ahead.

Stepping into the corporate office for the first time, Aarav felt a potent mixture of thrill and vulnerability. This was the moment he'd been waiting for—the opportunity he'd fought for with every ounce of his resolve. But self-doubt still lurked in the corners of his mind. Could he keep up with the demands of this new world? Would he be able to adapt, to prove himself?

As the day unfolded, he knew this marked the beginning of a new chapter, one promising both trials and rewards.

His first week at the airline office was a whirlwind of orientation sessions and rigorous training. Aarav felt like an outsider, constantly battling the nagging insecurity that he didn't belong. Surrounded by colleagues who seemed polished, poised, and effortlessly confident, he often wondered if he was cut out for this new life. Yet, amidst the chaos and uncertainty, there was one moment that stood out—a chance encounter that would linger in his mind, a spark that promised to change the course of his journey.

As he embraced this new chapter, Aarav couldn't help but feel tethered to the weight of his past. His family's expectations loomed large, a constant reminder of the sacrifices they had made to support his dreams. While his job at the airline was a source of pride for them, it also carried with it an unspoken burden—their hope that he would one day lift them out of their struggles and build a future that reflected their dreams, not just his.

Months into the job, Aarav began to sense that the airline wasn't his future. The routines, the corporate structures, and even the glimmer of ambition it offered failed to ignite the passion he craved. He felt restless, confined by a career that didn't align with the aspirations he had held onto for so long. After weeks of reflection, Aarav made a bold decision—he would prepare for the UPSC, the coveted civil services examination that promised not just prestige, but a chance to make a real difference.

However, the challenge of balancing his full-time job with his newfound ambition loomed large. Unable to join full-time coaching due to his work schedule, Aarav spent days researching the best ways to prepare on his own. He managed to gather UPSC notes from coaching institutes and bought an array of books, determined to dedicate three to four hours of study each night after returning home. Life became a delicate balancing act—working for the airline during the day, only to delve into the dense pages of political theory and governance by night. It was exhausting, but it gave him a sense of purpose, a light to guide him through the daily grind.

On weekends, Aarav often found himself returning to Bareilly, seeking refuge in the town's quiet familiarity. The pressure of living up to his family's dreams was always present, but in Bareilly, it felt bearable. The streets of Lucknow, where he worked, still felt foreign to him—he had no close friends, no companions with whom to spend his weekends. Bareilly, with its vibrant bazaars and the comfort of his roots, seemed like a balm to his soul, far removed from the corporate hustle and the cold anonymity of his office life.

Yet, Aarav knew he couldn't stay tethered to Bareilly forever. There was a restlessness within him, an inner voice pushing him toward something greater. He stood at a crossroads—caught between the simplicity and security of home and the thrilling but uncertain path that lay ahead. The allure of the city, with all its opportunities, beckoned him. But it was more than just ambition that drove him forward—it was the realization that his true journey was just beginning. The courage to chase his dreams was within reach; all he had to do was take the first step.

As the first chapter of his new life closed, Aarav stood on the cusp of something bigger than himself. The city waited, its doors open, its possibilities endless. And though the path ahead was fraught with challenges, he knew that the only way forward was to embrace the unknown, with all its risks and rewards. The journey had just begun.

Chapter 2: City Encounter

"The protagonist moves to the city for work, where he meets the 20-year-old girl, a city-bred, ambitious woman with a completely different outlook on life. They come from contrasting backgrounds, and their initial interactions are marked by curiosity and misunderstanding"

It was an ordinary afternoon in Aarav's office, the lull of post-lunch fatigue settling in. As was his routine, he decided to step out for a cup of tea, hoping the fresh air and the familiar warmth of chai would invigorate him. The sun hung lazily in the sky, casting soft shadows on the pavement as Aarav made his way to the street vendor, his thoughts drifting idly between work and the UPSC books waiting for him at home.

Just as he reached the exit, something caught his eye. A girl was walking toward the office entrance, her presence disrupting the humdrum of the day. Aarav slowed his pace, almost instinctively, and found himself standing still, watching her as she approached. There was something about her—a quiet grace in her steps, an air of confidence that set her apart from the usual office crowd.

Her hair swayed gently in the afternoon breeze, framing her face in soft waves. She walked with purpose, yet there was an ease in her movement, as if she belonged to a different rhythm, one that the bustling office world had yet to catch up with. Aarav's gaze followed her, drawn in by her simplicity and the effortless elegance with which she carried herself.

Aarav didn't know what it was—curiosity, intrigue, or something else altogether—but as she passed him by, he felt a stirring within, a feeling that perhaps this brief encounter was not as fleeting as it seemed. Aarav found himself rooted in place, watching her every step as she neared the entrance.

Forgetting all about his plan to go for tea, Aarav lingered at the office door, unable to pull his attention away. The familiar routine that usually marked his afternoons suddenly felt unimportant. The world outside could wait. He stood there, transfixed, as if time itself had slowed down just to allow him this moment.

He didn't go for tea that afternoon. Instead, he stayed right where he was, watching as she walked through the office doors, leaving behind an impression that would linger far longer than the few fleeting seconds of their encounter.

It was a Mahi who walked into the office, her presence immediately commanding attention. Standing at 5'6", she was tall and graceful, with a slim figure and a fair complexion that caught the light just right. Her long, straight hair framed her face, accentuating her glassy cheeks and bright black eyes that sparkled with ambition. Aarav couldn't help but notice her energy; she radiated a sense of purpose that both fascinated and intimidated him.

The moment she stepped inside, the atmosphere was different. The polished interiors, the crisp professionalism of the staff, and the aura of international grandeur enveloped her. This was the world she wanted to belong to. Mahi had come to drop off her CV for a position as a crew member. Aarav watched as she confidently approached the reception, her demeanor a stark contrast to his own self-doubt. After handing over her application, she turned to leave, but not before their eyes met. In that brief moment, Aarav felt an unexpected connection—an unspoken understanding that they were both chasing their dreams in this vast city.

As she left the office that day, the air felt lighter, filled with the possibility of change. Mahi knew that her journey was just beginning, but for the first time, it was a journey of her own making. She wasn't following the expectations of others—she was crafting her destiny. All she needed now was a chance, and she was ready to soar.

However, she soon discovered that the office was not authorized to hire flight crew directly. At the time, the airline was seeking trainees for a temporary assignment, and Mahi, along with several other candidates, was called for an interview.

Despite her initial hopes for a more permanent role, Mahi attended the interview, impressed by the professionalism of the process. Her intelligence and confidence shone through, and she successfully secured a spot in the program. However, when she learned that the internship was for just twenty-one days, she felt a wave of hesitation. A short-term position wasn't what she had envisioned for herself.

Yet, after considering the potential opportunities it could bring, Mahi changed her mind. She realized that this could be the stepping stone to something more—perhaps even a chance to prove her dedication and secure a full-time role in the airline. With that thought in mind, she decided to embrace the internship, hopeful that it would open new doors in her journey.

Who could have imagined that those mere *twenty-one days of training* would become the turning point for not just one, but two lives?

What seemed like a fleeting opportunity—a brief internship with no promise of permanence—would set in motion a series of events that neither Mahi nor

Aarav could foresee. For Mahi, the decision to step into this role wasn't just about professional growth, it was a leap into the unknown, driven by a hope that her future would hold more than what the present offered. Little did she know that it would also intertwine her path with someone who, at the time, was just another part of her story, but would soon become much more.

The training, though temporary, held the seeds of change. Those twenty-one days would prove to be the foundation for both their lives to evolve, drawing them into a journey neither had expected. It was the beginning of something that would soon transform into an uncharted chapter of love, ambition, and everything in between.

The following week, Mahi was offered a twenty-one-day internship at the airline, and fate twisted their paths once more. Aarav was tasked with helping to orient the new interns, and he soon found himself working closely with her. Their initial interactions were marked by a mix of curiosity and misunderstanding. Mahi was quick-witted and often sarcastic, while Aarav's responses were more reserved and thoughtful.

During lunch breaks, Mahi would recount stories of her life in the city, filled with aspirations of flying and adventure.

"As Mahi's academic journey was nothing short of remarkable. With over 90% marks in both her 10th and 12th grades from one of Lucknow's finest schools, she was the pride of her family. Her sharp intellect and dedication earned her a place in the Bachelor of Commerce program at the prestigious University of Lucknow, a natural step for someone as brilliant as her.

While pursuing her degree, Mahi set her sights on the banking sector. The grind of banking exam preparation didn't intimidate her. On the contrary, her focused mind and strong work ethic made her excel, and it came as no surprise when she cracked the State Bank of India (SBI) exam on her very first attempt. But the victory that should have brought celebration was soon overshadowed by family concerns. The job posting was in another state, far from the familiarity and safety of Lucknow, and her family's protective instincts flared. They did not allow her to join SBI, a decision that Mahi quietly accepted, even though it left her feeling restricted.

Determined not to let the setback define her, she embarked on a new path, turning her attention to Chartered Accountancy. Her family saw it as a secure and respectable profession, but for Mahi, the pursuit felt mechanical. The numbers, laws, and audits that she meticulously studied seemed to drain her spirit. She was a vibrant soul who craved more than just stability—she yearned for adventure. It didn't take long for her to realize that CA wasn't the future she *wanted. With little hesitation, she set the books aside, ready to pivot toward something that resonated with her heart.*

It was during this period of uncertainty that Mahi's inspiration arrived from an unexpected source. And, two of her closest friends had become air hostesses for international airlines. Every time they returned home, they carried with them stories of exotic cities, luxurious hotels, and the exhilarating lifestyle of traveling across continents to Mahi. Mahi listened, mesmerized by their experiences, and for the first time in a long while, she felt a spark of excitement. The independence and freedom they described ignited something within her. This was what she wanted—a career that offered her wings, both literally and figuratively"

She spoke passionately about her dream to become a flight attendant, the allure of the skies igniting her spirit and she had told Aarav listened, fascinated by her ambition. Mahi's dreams were painted in vivid colors, while his own felt muted in comparison.

"What about you, Aarav?" she asked one day, her gaze piercing through his carefully crafted facade. "What do you dream of?"

He hesitated, caught off guard by her directness. "I want to make a difference in the industry, I guess," he replied, trying to sound more certain than he felt.

"Just 'make a difference'?" Mahi teased, a smirk playing on her lips. "You need a bigger dream than that! Where's the adventure?"

Aarav chuckled nervously, feeling the weight of her expectations. "I suppose I haven't thought that far ahead. I'm just trying to get my footing."

Mahi's expression softened, and for a moment, he saw a flicker of empathy in her eyes. "We're all just trying to figure it out. But if you don't aim high, you'll never know how far you can go."

Their banter became a routine, filled with lighthearted jabs and shared laughter. Aarav began to appreciate Mahi's perspective—her optimism and fierce determination inspired him to reconsider his own aspirations. However, their differences also led to moments of misunderstanding. Aarav sometimes felt overshadowed by Mahi's confidence, struggling to assert himself in conversations.

One afternoon, as they walked back to the office after lunch, Mahi suddenly turned serious. "You know, I almost didn't apply here. My family's business collapsed a while back, and I was worried about what people would think of me."

Aarav paused, surprised. "I didn't know that. I guess we both have our struggles, huh?"

"Yeah," she said, a hint of vulnerability creeping into her voice. "But that's what drives me. I want to prove that I can rise above it. I want to fly."

Her words resonated deeply with Aarav. He understood the desire to break free from the constraints of their backgrounds. "I get that. My family has always depended on me to succeed. I feel like I have to carry their hopes."

Mahi nodded, her expression contemplative. "That pressure can be suffocating. But it can also be a catalyst for greatness. Use it to fuel your ambitions, not to hold you back."

As their internship progressed, Aarav found himself drawn to Mahi's ambition. She had a way of making even the mundane tasks exciting, and he admired her ability to connect with others effortlessly. Her enthusiasm was contagious, and slowly, Aarav began to shed some of his insecurities.

One evening, after a particularly challenging day, they found themselves at a coffee café day in Hazratganj, Lucknow, the air filled with the aroma of freshly brewed coffee. Mahi leaned back in her chair; her eyes sparkling. "So, what's next for you after the internship?"

"I'm not sure yet," Aarav admitted, swirling the dregs of his drink. "I just hope to find my place in the company."

"Find your place? Aarav, you should be carving your place! Make them see your potential. You've got to be bold."

Her words ignited a spark within him. For the first time, he felt a sense of clarity. Mahi's relentless drive reminded him that he had to push past his fears if he wanted to succeed.

As the weeks rolled by, the internship drew to a close. Mahi and Aarav had developed a bond, but it was still rooted in their contrasting backgrounds.

Part 2: Scenes

Chapter 3: Terms of Agreement

"A sudden twist brings them together under unusual circumstances—perhaps a project, a shared goal, or even a literal contract that forces them into a close working relationship. Despite their differences, they agree to work together, but with clear boundaries."

The days of the internship flowed seamlessly into one another, yet amidst the routine, something shifted within Aarav. He found himself increasingly captivated by Mahi. Her passion, determination, and vibrant spirit had drawn him in, and he started to notice the little things: the way her eyes sparkled when she talked about her dreams, the infectious laugh that brightened even the dullest of meetings. She was a force of nature, and he felt a magnetic pull toward her that he could no longer ignore.

Mahi, on her part, was also aware of Aarav's attention. She could feel his gaze lingering on her during team discussions, a warmth spreading through her whenever their eyes met. But she remained uncertain about how to approach the burgeoning feelings between them. Their interactions were light and playful, yet there was an unspoken tension that both excited and unnerved her.

Then, one Thursday morning, the unexpected happened. Mahi's mother was rushed to the hospital due to a sudden emergency, leaving Mahi grappling with fear and uncertainty. In her distress, she neglected to inform her supervisors about her absence, causing a stir in the office. Aarav's heart sank when he realized Mahi hadn't been around for two days.

His immediate supervisor approached him with a concerned expression. "Aarav, do you know where Mahi is? She hasn't come to the office, and no one seems to have heard from her."

Panic set in. This was not just a professional concern; it was deeply personal for him. Aarav felt a surge of urgency. He had been waiting for an opportunity to connect with her on a deeper level, and now, the stakes felt higher than ever. With a mix of hope and anxiety swirling within him, he decided to call her.

Dialing her number, Aarav's heart raced. What would he say? Would he come off as too intrusive? After what felt like an eternity, Mahi answered. Her voice was barely a whisper, filled with weariness. "Yes, sir?"

"Mahi, it's Aarav. I wanted to check on you. Is everything okay?" he asked, his concern palpable.

There was a brief pause before she replied, her voice trembling slightly. "My mother is in the hospital.

It's serious," she admitted, the gravity of her situation sinking in.

Aarav's heart ached for her. "I'm so sorry to hear that. If there's anything you need—anything at all—please let me know," he urged, feeling the weight of her distress.

"Thank you for asking, Aarav. I really appreciate it," she said softly. They exchanged a few more words, but the conversation felt heavy, filled with unspoken worries and emotions.

Eventually, they disconnected, and Aarav was left with a lingering sense of helplessness.

That same day, as Aarav sat at his desk, his thoughts drifted back to Mahi. He felt compelled to reach out again, to express his support more directly. After a restless evening of mulling over his words, he finally mustered the courage to text her.

"Are you okay? Is your mother doing better? If you need any help, please don't hesitate to ask," he typed, pouring his genuine concern into each word before hitting send. It felt like a leap of faith.

But fate had other plans. Mahi's phone had died, and she didn't see his message that night. Aarav found himself restless, checking his phone repeatedly for a notification, each ping igniting a flicker of hope. Hours passed, and when he finally drifted off to sleep, it was with a heavy heart, tinged with worry for her.

The next morning, the first rays of sunlight filtered through his window, heralding a new day. Just as he prepared for another day at the office, his phone rang. It was Mahi.

"Hello?" he answered, surprised but hopeful.

"Aarav, I'm sorry for not getting back to you. My mother is stable now, but it was a tough night," she said, her voice still shaky but more grounded than before.

Relief flooded through him. "I'm so glad to hear that. I was really worried about you. I wanted to make sure you were okay."

"Thank you for checking on me," Mahi replied, her tone softening. "It means a lot."

They talked for a few more minutes, sharing snippets about the hospital visit. Aarav felt an unexpected bond forming—a deeper connection forged in shared concerns and vulnerability. In those moments, the walls they had both erected began to crumble, revealing glimpses of their true selves.

By the end of the call, they agreed to meet later that day to discuss their current project, a task that had suddenly taken on new significance. Aarav felt a mixture of anticipation and anxiety as they planned their collaboration. This meeting would not just be about work; it would be a chance for them to solidify their budding relationship.

As they settled into a conference room that evening, the atmosphere felt charged with potential. Mahi's vibrant energy seemed to fill the space, and Aarav couldn't help but admire her tenacity. They began discussing the project, brainstorming ideas and strategies. The synergy between them was palpable; their thoughts intertwined effortlessly, and laughter punctuated their discussions.

"Let's set some ground rules," Mahi suggested, her eyes sparkling with mischief. "We can be friends and colleagues, but no distractions. We have a project to complete."

Aarav nodded, appreciating her directness. "Agreed. We'll keep it professional."

Yet, deep down, both understood that the lines between friendship and something more were beginning to blur. As they dived into their project, their dynamic evolved—each meeting charged with an undercurrent of unspoken feelings. The tension simmered beneath the surface, electrifying the air between them but from the very first moment Mahi stepped into the airline office, Aarav felt something stir within him. It wasn't just a passing glance or a fleeting attraction—it was as if the world had tilted ever so slightly, drawing his attention to her in a way he couldn't ignore. She walked into the office that day with quiet confidence, her presence illuminating the otherwise ordinary surroundings. Aarav, who had never believed in such things as love at first sight, found himself captivated.

At first, he dismissed it as nothing more than a simple crush—something fleeting that would fade with time. But as the days turned into weeks, Aarav realized this was something deeper, something that grew every time he saw her. The way she smiled when she greeted someone, the soft tone of her voice when she spoke, and the effortless grace with which she carried herself—each moment spent in her presence only intensified his feelings. What began as a crush had quietly blossomed into a quiet, unspoken affection.

There was something about Mahi that felt different. She wasn't just beautiful, though that alone was enough to catch anyone's attention. There was a warmth to her, a quiet determination in her eyes, and a spark of passion in the way she approached life. Aarav couldn't help but be drawn to that, and with time, his crush transformed into something far more profound. It wasn't just her physical presence that captivated him—it was everything she represented. Her kindness, her ambition, and her unspoken strength resonated with him, stirring emotions he hadn't known were there.

But despite the intensity of his feelings, Aarav knew it was far too early to confess. He kept his emotions tightly guarded, wearing a mask of casual indifference whenever they crossed paths. Each time she passed by his desk or their conversations flowed into light banter, Aarav felt his heart race. But he remained silent, choosing to hide his emotions behind polite smiles and friendly gestures, fearing that revealing the depth of his affection might push her away or disrupt the fragile connection they had.

Every glance, every brief moment they shared in the office, made his feelings grow. Aarav would often catch himself stealing glances when he thought no one was watching, his heart swelling with a tenderness he didn't know how to express. He was falling in love with Mahi—slowly, deeply, and with a quiet intensity that surprised him. But he knew that, for now, he had to keep his feelings to himself. It wasn't the right time. So, he stayed silent, allowing his heart to speak through stolen moments and lingering looks, hoping that someday, when the moment was right, he could finally tell her the truth.

For now, though, Aarav was content with watching from afar, cherishing every small interaction and holding onto the hope that one day, he would be able to tell Mahi just how deeply he had fallen for her.

In the following days, they became each other's sounding boards, sharing not only ideas but also personal anecdotes. Mahi confided in Aarav about her family's struggles, the weight of expectations she carried. Aarav opened up about his own fears and aspirations, the pressure he felt to succeed and support his family back in Bareilly.

Through these conversations, they discovered common ground. Both had experienced the challenges of growing up in middle-class families, grappling with societal expectations while nurturing their dreams. The vulnerability they shared began to forge a deeper connection, transforming their partnership into something more significant.

One evening, as they worked late to finalize their project, Mahi looked up from her notes. "You know, Aarav, I never expected to find such a strong ally in this internship. You've really pushed me to think bigger."

He smiled, warmth spreading through him. "I feel the same way. You've inspired me to step out of my comfort zone."

The moment hung in the air, a silent acknowledgment of the bond that was forming. It was clear that both were beginning to see each other as more than just colleagues; there was an undeniable chemistry that danced just beneath the surface.

However, they both understood the importance of maintaining boundaries. Mahi was determined to focus on her career, and Aarav, still finding his footing, was hesitant to complicate things. They agreed to keep their relationship strictly professional, yet as the days turned into weeks, the tension became harder to ignore.

With the project successfully completed, the culmination of their hard work was celebrated in the office. Mahi beamed as she received praise for her contributions, and Aarav felt a swell of pride for her. They stood together, reveling in the moment, their chemistry palpable.

As the celebration wound down, Aarav felt a mix of exhilaration and uncertainty. He wanted to express his feelings but feared jeopardizing the connection they had built. Instead, they exchanged a knowing glance, both aware that something deeper lingered between them.

"One Romantic Evening"

It was a fine evening, the kind that promised memories and whispered possibilities. The sky was painted in shades of deep indigo, punctuated by the twinkling stars that adorned the 11th October 2011, Purnima night. Aarav and Mahi had just wrapped up a long, demanding day at the office. Their laughter lingered in the quiet corridors as they stepped outside, the cool night air brushing gently against their faces. The city around them seemed to exhale, slowing down as dusk settled into the embrace of night.

Mahi, her eyes sparkling under the soft streetlights, glanced at Aarav, her curiosity piqued. "Where do you live in Lucknow?" she asked, her voice casual but laced with a hint of playfulness.

Aarav smiled, tilting his head slightly, as if the question amused him. "I live near Gomti Nagar," he replied, his tone easy, yet there was an undertone of warmth.

Mahi suddenly stopped walking and turned to face him, a flicker of mischief dancing in her eyes. "Let's go," she said impulsively, her lips curving into a soft smile. "I just want to see where you live." The surprise in Aarav's eyes mirrored the leap his heart made at her unexpected request. He hadn't anticipated this – the thought of her standing in the space where his everyday life unfolded felt intimate, personal. Aarav turned to Mahi; his face soft with an amused smile as they strolled under the quiet night sky. His eyes gleamed with a playful mischief, making the moment feel lighter, almost teasing.

"Mahi, I can't take you to my place," Aarav said in a polite but jesting tone, his voice carrying a certain charm that always made her smile. He paused for effect, letting the humor of his words sink in. "Girls aren't allowed in the building."

Mahi raised an eyebrow, her lips twitching as she tried to hold back a laugh. "Oh, is that so?" she responded, her voice teasing, matching his playful mood. "Or is it just a convenient excuse to keep me out of your secret world?"

Mahi's face lit up with determination. "Oh, come on! I just want to see where you live. It's not a big deal! Please?" Her insistence made Aarav chuckle.

With a teasing sigh, he finally relented. "Alright, let's go, but just for a little while."

As they walked through the posh colony, Aarav felt a mix of excitement and nervousness. He lived in a small, modest room, a far cry from the vibrant energy that Mahi radiated. He pushed the door open, revealing the sparse yet cozy space, and immediately went to make ginger tea—Mahi's favorite.

"Ginger tea? You remember?" Aarav asked, glancing over his shoulder with a smile.

Of course! It's the best," she replied, her eyes twinkling as she settled into the small, slightly worn-out chair.

They shared stories and laughter over steaming cups of tea, the world outside fading away. Time slipped by unnoticed, and soon they decided to take a stroll under the stars. The moonlight bathed the path in a silvery glow as they wandered, the atmosphere electric with unspoken feelings.

"What's your plan for the future, Aarav?" Mahi asked, breaking the comfortable silence.

Aarav chuckled, shaking his head. "Honestly, I don't have a big plan. I just want to stick with this job for now."

Mahi narrowed her eyes playfully. "Oh no, that laugh tells me you're hiding something. You must have a dream!"

With a mock-serious expression, Aarav finally confessed, "Alright, fine. I dream with open eyes about qualifying for UPSC and becoming an IAS officer."

Mahi's eyes widened, and a bright smile broke across her face. "That's an amazing dream! I can totally see you as a leader!"

Feeling buoyed by her enthusiasm, Aarav decided to turn the tables. "And what about you, Mahi? What's your plan?"

Her smile faded slightly, replaced by a hint of vulnerability. "What can I plan right now? I'm just happy to be doing this internship that pays a mere hundred dollars. As a B.com first-year student, what more can I expect?"

Aarav noticed the emotion welling up in her eyes, and his heart ached for her. "I'm sorry, I shouldn't have asked. I didn't mean to upset you."

Mahi brushed it off, but the sadness lingered. "It's fine. I'm used to it," she replied, her voice barely above a whisper.

Aarav felt a surge of protectiveness. Without thinking, he reached for her hand, intertwining his fingers with hers. It was a simple gesture, but it sent a ripple of warmth through both of them. Mahi looked up, her eyes glistening, and before he knew it, she hugged him tightly.

As Aarav held Mahi close, time seemed to dissolve around them. Her breath was warm against his chest, her fingers clasped tightly on his shirt, holding on as though letting go would leave her vulnerable to the harsh world they had temporarily escaped. The distant sounds of the city faded, replaced by the soft hum of their shared silence. For Mahi, this embrace was a rare surrender, a moment to let down her guard after years of being strong and carrying her dreams and disappointments alone.

Aarav felt the weight of her sadness, an invisible burden she carried so well that even he had missed it before tonight. He realized that beneath her confident demeanor was a vulnerability she rarely let anyone see. This was the Mahi who carried her struggles silently, who smiled through lonely nights and ambitious days, and who bore the weight of her dreams without asking for help. And now, she had trusted him enough to see this fragile side of her, to lean on him even if only for a moment.

"I'm here, Mahi. You don't have to do this alone," he whispered, his hand moving in gentle circles along her back, hoping his touch could somehow communicate the words his heart couldn't express.

Mahi looked up, her face softened in the dim light, her eyes glistening with unshed tears and something else, something unspoken that lingered between them. "Thank you, Aarav. I didn't realize how much I needed someone just to listen." Her voice was barely above a whisper, as if the admission itself might vanish if spoken any louder.

Her vulnerability tugged at something deep within him. He brought his hand to her face, softly brushing away the trace of a tear with his thumb. "You deserve so much more than loneliness, Mahi. You've been there for everyone—let someone be there for you."

She closed her eyes, breathing in his words, and for a moment, she let herself believe in them. When her eyes opened, they held a quiet intensity, a look that both welcomed and challenged him. There was an undeniable connection, a magnetic pull that seemed to draw them closer, despite the invisible line they had never dared to cross.

Aarav hesitated, his heart pounding with the weight of unspoken feelings. He took a deep breath and leaned in, pressing a gentle, lingering kiss to her forehead. It wasn't a kiss filled with grand gestures or spoken confessions but one of comfort and silent promises, one that acknowledged the depth of their bond. In that kiss, he poured everything he had felt, everything he had wanted to say, into a single, silent moment of devotion.

Mahi's breath caught, and she felt a surge of warmth and belonging. The kiss, tender yet powerful, seemed to melt the invisible walls she had built around herself. She tightened her arms around him, feeling the steady beat of his heart against her cheek, grounding her, giving her a sense of peace she had longed for but never dared to hope for.

As they stood in each other's arms, the city lights twinkling around them, a shared silence blanketed them—a silence that held both the weight of unspoken words and the comfort of mutual understanding. They felt a sense of timelessness as if they were the only two people in the world, cocooned in a shared warmth that neither wanted to break.

"Are you okay now?" Aarav's voice was barely a murmur, filled with genuine care and concern.

"Yes," she replied softly, her voice filled with an unexpected confidence. In this embrace, she felt seen, held, and understood. "I think...I think I finally am." She looked up at him, her eyes shining with gratitude and something deeper, something she hadn't fully acknowledged herself.

For a moment, they simply looked at each other, the air thick with possibilities. Aarav's hand moved to her cheek again, tracing gentle lines as if trying to memorize her face, every feature, every emotion etched into her expression. His heart raced, and he fought the urge to pull her closer, to let his feelings pour out in words he had long kept hidden. But words felt unnecessary, almost too fragile to carry the intensity of what he felt.

She gave a small, tentative smile, her own eyes searching his as if seeking permission, validation, an answer to the question she hadn't dared to ask. The world around them blurred, their hearts beating in sync as they held each other in the delicate, electrifying tension that had woven itself between them. It was a promise, an unsaid agreement that they both felt but couldn't name.

Aarav leaned forward once more, this time his face inches from hers, close enough to feel her breath against his lips. There was a pause, a moment of silent anticipation where they both hovered at the edge, waiting, unsure yet so certain in the shared desire.

But then, almost instinctively, they held back. Not out of fear but out of respect for the delicate beauty of what had just passed between them. They understood the depth of their emotions without needing to express them in grand declarations.

Instead, Aarav wrapped his arms around her once more, pulling her close in a protective embrace, one that held all his unsaid feelings, all the love, admiration, and respect he had for her. He wanted her to know, without a shadow of a doubt, that he would always be there for her, a steady presence in her life, a silent supporter of her dreams and struggles.

In his arms, Mahi felt her walls crumble entirely. She realized she didn't have to carry everything alone, that there was someone willing to share her burdens, her dreams, her fears. And in that moment, she allowed herself to believe in a future where she didn't have to be alone, where she could lean on someone without feeling weak, where she could love and be loved in return.

Under the blanket of stars, in the quiet night, they found a shared understanding that words couldn't capture.

But in that fleeting second, the kiss transformed. The warmth of the moment ignited something deeper, and he found himself leaning in closer, their lips finally meeting.

It was soft, tentative at first, but as the world around them faded, the kiss deepened. Aarav felt a rush of emotions—joy, fear, and an exhilarating sense of connection. Time stood still as they lost themselves in that single moment, the outside world disappearing into a blur of starlight.

After what felt like an eternity, they pulled away, breathless, eyes wide with surprise and wonder. Mahi's cheeks flushed a soft pink, and she looked at Aarav as if he had just opened a door to an entirely new realm. But then, as quickly as it had begun, she gathered her things, her expression shifting from exhilaration to confusion.

"I— I have to go," she stammered, her voice shaky. She grabbed her bag and keys, her movements hurried.

"Mahi, wait—" Aarav started, but she was already at the door.

Without another word, she slipped out into the night, leaving Aarav standing alone in his small room, the warmth of their kiss still lingering on his lips. The silence enveloped him, and an unexpected wave of panic washed over him. Did she not like it? Was it too soon?

He dialled her number repeatedly, each ring echoing the uncertainty that had begun to creep into his heart. But every attempt met with silence. His stomach twisted in knots, anxiety clawing at him.

After hours of restless waiting, he finally sent her a message, pouring out his feelings: I'm so sorry if I made you uncomfortable. I didn't mean to rush things. I hope you're okay. The minutes dragged on, each second feeling like an eternity until finally, a notification popped up on his screen.

It was Mahi.

Tonight was magical. I just needed some time to process. 😊

Relief flooded through him, mixed with a rush of happiness. He quickly typed back, I'm glad you felt that way. Can we talk tomorrow?

Her response was instantaneous. Of course! Can't wait to see you again!

As he set his phone down, Aarav felt a smile stretch across his face. He knew that this was just the beginning of something beautiful. They had crossed a threshold, one that promised growth and deeper understanding. It was a moment etched in time—a first kiss that was more than just a gesture; it was the spark that ignited a new chapter in their journey together.

In the weeks that followed, their partnership continued to flourish, but the unspoken feelings lingered in the air, leaving both Aarav and Mahi to navigate their emotions carefully. They were at a crossroads—two ambitious individuals from different backgrounds, united by their dreams but hesitant to cross that line into something more.

As they moved forward, Aarav couldn't help but reflect on the whirlwind of change that had swept into his life since Mahi entered it. With her by his side, he felt a renewed sense of purpose, a drive to not only excel in his work but also to confront his emotions. The journey ahead was uncertain, but with Mahi's influence, he was ready to embrace whatever lay ahead. Would they remain just colleagues, or was something deeper waiting to unfold? Only time would tell. Their final days of the internship approached, and Aarav couldn't ignore the sense of impending change. Mahi had made it clear that she wanted to continue pursuing her ambitions in the airline industry, but Aarav remained uncertain about his path. Would he have the courage to embrace the possibilities that lay ahead?

On the last day of the internship, they gathered with their colleagues to celebrate their achievements. Mahi beamed as she received praise for her hard work, and Aarav felt a swell of pride for her. As they stood side by side, he turned to her. "You've really inspired me, Mahi."

"Good! Just remember to keep aiming high," she replied, her eyes sparkling with determination.

As the celebration wound down, Aarav made a decision. He would not let his circumstances define him. With Mahi's influence and the lessons, he had learned during the internship, he was ready to embrace his future.

When it was time to say goodbye, Aarav felt a pang of sadness. They had become unlikely friends, united by their dreams and struggles. "I'll miss this," he admitted, looking at Mahi.

"Don't be a stranger, Aarav. Let's keep in touch. You never know where life will take us," she said, her smile infectious.

As he walked away, Aarav felt a newfound sense of purpose. The city, once overwhelming, now felt like a place of opportunity. With Mahi's encouragement, he was ready to chase his dreams, ready to take flight. Their paths might have diverged, but the impact she had made on his life would stay with him forever.

Aarav took a deep breath, the city air filling his lungs with promise. It was time to embrace his journey, to rise above his fears and soar into the future he had always dreamed of.

The cacophony of honking horns and bustling crowds pressed in from all sides, stirring an anxious knot in his stomach. Yet amidst the overwhelming rush of the city, there was a flicker of exhilaration. This wasn't just a new place—it was the threshold of a new chapter. A chapter that held challenges he had never faced, and opportunities he had long dreamed of. With a deep breath, Aarav gathered his thoughts and stepped forward, ready to embrace whatever came next.

Chapter 4: A Leap of Faith

"When Love Hangs in the Balance"

As the internship ended, the rhythm of Aarav and Mahi's world shifted. What had once been near-daily encounters and familiar silences had turned into fleeting moments—rare, brief meetings that held the weight of a thousand unspoken words. Now, they could only steal a few hours once or twice a week, tethered instead to messages and midnight calls, each conversation a thread that kept them connected despite the growing distance.

But as days turned into weeks, Aarav found himself yearning for more than just words on a screen or voices carried through a line. The clarity in his heart had grown undeniable; he could no longer ignore the feelings that stirred within him. Mahi had become more than a friend, more than a confidante. She had quietly slipped into the corners of his heart, filling spaces he hadn't known were empty. Finally, one evening, as a blush-colored dusk blanketed the city, Aarav decided he could wait no longer. He began to plan a confession that would bring his feelings out of the shadows and into the light. He imagined every word, the way he'd look into her eyes, the courage he'd need to overcome his lingering fears of vulnerability and rejection. He rehearsed, only to stumble, in the solitude of his room, his thoughts like a nervous rhythm in his chest. Aarav had planned something special, something that would either bring them closer together or create a distance he feared to imagine.

He had chosen the Capaccino Blast restaurant in Gomti Nagar, Lucknow, as the setting for his confession. It was a quaint place, known for its cozy ambiance and excellent coffee—perfect for the kind of intimate conversation he was hoping for. As Aarav waited in his office that Saturday afternoon, his heart was a storm of emotions. Mahi had agreed to meet him, but there was an undeniable tension in the air, and Aarav found himself battling a swarm of 'what ifs' that threatened to overwhelm him.

When Mahi arrived on her Scooty, the sight of her immediately calmed his nerves, if only slightly. Dressed casually in her favorite pastel shades, her hair pulled back in a loose ponytail, Mahi looked every bit like the woman he had come to admire—fierce, independent, and kind. Aarav climbed onto the back of her Scooty, the hum of the engine filling the silence as they navigated the bustling streets of Lucknow.

As they rode, Aarav's mind wandered. *What if she says no? What if this changes everything? What if she stops talking to me?* The fear gnawed at him, making the fifteen-minute ride feel like an eternity. He wanted this moment to be perfect, but the uncertainty of her response weighed heavily on his heart.

Finally, they reached the restaurant, its warm lights casting a comforting glow as they walked inside. They chose a corner table, secluded enough for the conversation Aarav had been rehearsing in his mind for days. After ordering coffee and sandwiches, the conversation flowed easily at first—casual updates about their lives and the usual banter that came so naturally between them. But Aarav's nervousness was palpable.

Suddenly, Mahi looked up, her brow furrowing slightly, her eyes searching his with a mixture of curiosity and concern. The playful banter seemed to melt away as a more serious tone entered her voice.

As the sun dipped below the horizon, casting a warm, amber glow through the windows of the quiet café, Aarav and Mahi sat across from each other, their hands almost close enough to touch. The soft hum of background chatter and the gentle clinking of coffee cups created a soothing ambiance, but neither seemed to notice, wrapped in the intensity of the moment.

"Aarav," Mahi began, her gaze tender and questioning. "Why did you ask me to meet today?" She tilted her head slightly, her hair catching the light. "We just met yesterday. Is something going on?"

He took a deep breath, feeling the familiar warmth that Mahi's presence always seemed to awaken within him. For weeks, he had rehearsed this conversation in his mind, each detail meticulously envisioned. Yet now, under her gentle scrutiny, words felt fragile, like petals trembling in the wind. He looked down at his hands clasped together under the table, as if searching for courage in the folds of his fingers.

"Yes, Mahi," he said, his voice a little strained, tinged with the weight of unspoken feelings. "There's something I've been wanting to tell you."

Mahi's gaze softened, a hint of concern flickering across her face as she leaned forward, eyes intent. There was something vulnerable in Aarav's expression that made her heart beat faster. She held her breath, waiting, a thousand questions shimmering in her mind.

Aarav's gaze finally rose to meet hers, and she could see the depth of emotion reflected in his eyes. "I've been thinking about this for a while," he continued, his voice hushed yet steady. "I don't know how else to say it, but...I've fallen in love with you, Mahi."

The words hung between them, fragile yet powerful, like a declaration etched into the evening air. He watched her closely, his heart racing, as he reached across the table, his fingers brushing lightly against hers. For a moment, there was only silence – a silence filled with longing, fear, and hope.

Aarav looked away, breaking the spell, and took another breath. "You've become this... this light in my life, Mahi. And every day, I find myself wondering what it would be like to have you by my side. I don't just want to be close to you," he whispered, voice trembling. "I want to build a life with you."

Mahi's expression softened, her eyes reflecting both surprise and something deeper, something that words couldn't quite capture. She opened her mouth, as if to say something, but her voice seemed caught in the swell of emotions swirling inside her. Instead, she just held his gaze, a slow smile spreading across her face, her cheeks flushed.

Aarav felt a wave of relief wash over him at her unspoken response, the weight of his confession lifting as her hand rested in his. He closed his fingers around hers, as though sealing a promise within that touch.

There it was—the truth, raw and vulnerable, laid out between them like an open wound. Aarav's heart raced as he watched her reaction, trying to gauge what she might be feeling. She blinked, taken aback, her expression a mixture of surprise and confusion.

He continued; his voice softer now. "I know this might come as a shock, and I don't expect you to give me an answer right away. But I couldn't keep these feelings inside any longer. I care about you deeply, Mahi, and I want you to know that."

Aarav reached into his bag and pulled out a small gift—some shirts and t-shirts he had chosen for her. Mahi hesitated, her initial instinct to refuse the gift, but Aarav gently insisted.

"Please, Mahi, this is just a token of my feelings. If nothing else, consider it a gesture of my respect for you."

Mahi looked down at the neatly wrapped package, her hands trembling slightly. She was silent for a long moment, her eyes flitting between Aarav and the gift. Finally, she accepted it with a soft nod. "Thank you," she whispered, her voice barely audible. "I...I need some time to think."

Aarav nodded, understanding the weight of her words. He hadn't expected an immediate answer, but the uncertainty gnawed at him all the same. They finished their meal in relative silence, the easy rapport they once shared now tinged with an unspoken tension. When it was time to leave, Mahi offered to drop Aarav back at his place, as she always did.

As they rode through the dimly lit streets of Lucknow, Aarav felt the weight of the evening settle on his shoulders. The night was cool, the wind whipping through his hair as they sped through the traffic, but his thoughts were consumed by Mahi's reaction. *What if she decides not to speak to me again? What if I've ruined everything?*

When they arrived at his apartment, Mahi gave him a small smile, though it didn't reach her eyes. "I'll see you later, Aarav," she said, her voice gentle but distant. Aarav nodded, watching her drive away, a hollow feeling in his chest. That night, sleep eluded him. His mind kept replaying the evening, wondering if he had made the right decision, wondering if he had lost her forever.

The silence over the next few days felt heavier than any moment Aarav had ever experienced. Each time his phone buzzed, a mix of excitement and apprehension stirred inside him, only to feel the weight of disappointment when it wasn't her. Their conversations had grown distant, almost business-like, and Mahi's reserved replies tore at his heart. But Aarav stayed patient, giving her the space he knew she needed, even as hope became both his solace and his torment.

On the third day, as he lay in bed replaying their last meeting in his mind, his thoughts wavered between optimism and self-doubt. He could still see her, standing beside him that evening, her eyes a blend of wonder and uncertainty. The soft cadence of her voice echoed in his ears as he drifted off to sleep, and he couldn't help but smile, despite the gnawing suspense.

By the fifth day, Aarav could hardly focus on work. The people around him seemed a blur, and every task felt like a mountain. Colleagues commented on his distraction, but he just laughed it off, hiding the storm brewing inside him. He began to fear that his love might remain unreturned. Yet, each morning, he dressed with care, almost as if he were preparing for the moment, she might call him and end this waiting game.

Then, on the sixth day, late in the evening, his phone finally rang. Her name appeared on the screen, and his pulse raced as he picked up, trying to sound calm. He heard a slight hesitation in her voice, as if she, too, was holding back a tide of emotions.

"Aarav," she began, her tone soft, almost tender. "I've been thinking a lot about what you said... and about us."

The words hung in the air, filling him with both relief and anticipation. Her voice trembled slightly, and he could feel the depth of her thoughts, her vulnerability hidden behind her steady words. He took a deep breath, ready for whatever was to come.

"Aarav, I want to be yours," she whispered, the words flowing as though they were waiting to be said. "I've been scared, unsure of what this might mean for us, but I've realized that I feel the same way. I love you, Aarav."

Aarav's breath caught in his throat. It was as if the world had paused, every sound fading, leaving just her words lingering in the air. He could barely believe what he was hearing, but the softness in her tone reassured him that this was real, that this was everything he'd been waiting for.

"Mahi... you have no idea what this means to me," he managed, his voice trembling with emotion. "I've loved you, every part of you, and I'll spend my life proving that to you. Thank you... for trusting me, for letting us happen."

Relief, joy, and a flood of emotions washed over Aarav as her words sank in. He could hardly believe it— she had said yes.

In that moment, everything fell into place. The uncertainty, the sleepless nights, the nervous anticipation—it had all led to this. As Aarav smiled into the phone, a new chapter in their story began, one filled with the promise of love, understanding, and the hope of a future they would build together.

Chapter 5: Clashing Worlds

"Their differences in background, values, and personalities start creating friction. The boy struggles to adjust to city life and the girl's fast-paced, independent lifestyle.

As the days turned into weeks, the initial excitement of their relationship began to reveal the cracks between Aarav and Mahi. What had once felt like a seamless partnership started to strain under the weight of their contrasting worlds. The vibrant city of Lucknow, with its relentless ambition and fast pace, became a battleground for their differences.

Aarav, from the modest streets of Bareilly, struggled with the pressures of city life. The honking horns, bustling crowds, and endless rush felt suffocating. The city, once a symbol of his dreams, now loomed over him, making him feel small and uncertain. Mahi, however, thrived in this environment. Her confidence and independence radiated in every action, creating an undeniable contrast to Aarav's quiet hesitations.

One late afternoon, while Aarav was hunched over his desk, lost in paperwork under the soft glow of his office lamp, his phone buzzed. It was Mahi. Her voice held an unexpected mix of excitement and warmth, "Aarav, how about visiting my parents this weekend? I think it's time you met them." Her words lingered, hinting at the deeper step they were about to take. Aarav's heart quickened, realizing how much this meeting meant to her. "Of course," he replied softly, feeling a blend of anticipation and gratitude.

That weekend, Aarav dressed with care, feeling both nervous and honored as he made his way to Mahi's family home. The moment he stepped inside, he was enveloped in warmth and hospitality. Mahi's parents welcomed him with open arms, treating him less like a guest and more like someone they had known forever. Her mother had even prepared his favorite *Rajma-Rice*, a thoughtful touch that instantly made him feel at ease. The room buzzed with stories, laughter, and the aroma of familiar spices, creating a sense of intimacy that softened the edges of his nerves.

As the evening unfolded, Aarav found himself exchanging stories and laughter with Mahi's family, gradually embracing the sense of belonging they offered. When it was time to leave, he lingered, savoring the comfort of the evening before finally turning to Mahi. "So, how do your parents feel?" he asked, his voice betraying a trace of vulnerability.

With a soft smile and a gleam in her eyes, Mahi replied, "They loved you. They think you're kind, respectful... and just the right kind of simple." Her words wrapped around him like a promise, deepening his resolve.

After that visit, something shifted between them. They began to meet more frequently, exploring Lucknow's vibrant streets with a new sense of closeness. Yet, as time passed, the quiet tension between their worlds grew harder to ignore, the differences between their dreams and realities casting subtle shadows on their moments together. Still, they continued, caught between love and the quiet whisper of unspoken challenges.

The quiet bond between Aarav and Mahi grew into something more during their frequent explorations around Lucknow. Each alley they walked, every chai stall they visited, every sunset they watched together—these moments became subtle threads weaving them closer. Yet, as time wore on, the challenges began to cast shadows over their relationship.

Mahi often pushed Aarav to meet her friends and expand his circle, hoping he'd adapt to the city's social pulse, but Aarav's life was tightly packed. Between his job, UPSC preparations, and tutoring to manage his education loan and support his family, Aarav barely had any time to spare. Each evening ended in exhaustion, and his schedule left little room for socializing or even just a carefree evening with Mahi.

One evening, as Aarav wrapped up yet another tutoring session, his phone vibrated with a message from Mahi: "Meet me at our spot, please?" It was late, and fatigue clouded his mind, but he knew Mahi's tone well enough to understand that this wasn't just a simple request.

He found her waiting at a small café they often frequented. Mahi looked up as he approached, her face a mixture of frustration and concern.

"Aarav, I feel like every time I try to involve you in my life, you shut me out," she said, her voice trembling slightly. "Why won't you meet my friends? I know you're busy, but these connections... they matter. To both of us."

Aarav sighed, struggling to find the words. "Mahi, it's not that I don't want to meet your friends or spend more time with you. I just... I have responsibilities. After work, it's UPSC prep, then tutoring so I can pay off the loan and support my family. I'm stretched thin."

"But, Aarav," Mahi insisted, "you can't just live like this, always sacrificing everything for your responsibilities. What about you? Your dreams, your happiness... doesn't that count too?"

Her words struck a chord within him. Aarav's dream of clearing UPSC and building a better life for his family weighed heavily on him, and even his time with Mahi often felt like a stolen luxury. He looked at her, eyes pained. "I want to do this for myself too, Mahi. But right now, I don't have the luxury of ignoring my responsibilities."

Frustration flared up in Mahi's eyes. "Aarav, life isn't just about responsibilities. Don't you realize how much you're missing out on? You're so focused on tomorrow that you're forgetting to live today."

Their words hung in the air, unspoken emotions filling the silence between them. Mahi's frustration was genuine; she wanted Aarav to be part of her world, to share her life in the present, not just in moments they managed to steal.

But for Aarav, this was a reality he couldn't escape. Every day was a tightrope walk, balancing his dreams and his duties. He had no choice but to keep pushing forward, even if it meant sacrificing parts of his life that other people might take for granted.

This moment of tension marked a turning point between them. They both knew they were standing at the crossroads of two vastly different worlds—Aarav, with his singular, driven focus on making a better life, and Mahi, with her desire for togetherness, spontaneity, and the small joys of life shared.

And yet, despite the pull of these opposing worlds, they found themselves drawn to each other, unable to let go. For every painful silence and unspoken disagreement, there was an unshakable bond. The love they shared carried them through each struggle, each sacrifice, but at what cost?

Aarav sighed, feeling the weight of her expectations. "I just don't feel comfortable in those settings, Mahi," he said, his voice quiet but firm. "I come from a different background. These fancy parties, the small talk—they're not really my scene."

Mahi crossed her arms, her face a mix of exasperation and worry. "But you have to put yourself out there! You're so capable, but how will people see that if you don't show them? You can't stay in your comfort zone forever."

Aarav's frustration grew, feeling as though she couldn't understand his struggle. "I believe in myself, Mahi. But that doesn't mean I have to change who I am to fit into this world of yours. I'm not made for these social circles, these high-paced lifestyles. It's just... not me."

Their arguments grew more frequent. Every clash felt like a widening gap between their two worlds, pulling them further apart. Aarav, feeling out of place in the city, often longed for the simplicity of Bareilly. Mahi, fiercely independent and determined to make a mark in the city, couldn't understand why Aarav hesitated to embrace her lifestyle.

In an effort to bridge the growing distance between them, Mahi invited Aarav to a gathering at her friend's home one weekend. She hoped that, by exposing him more to her life in Lucknow, he might begin to feel more at ease. Aarav reluctantly agreed, his anxiety simmering just below the surface.

When he arrived at her friend's apartment, the stark difference between his life and hers hit him again. The space was modern, sleek, and filled with the latest gadgets. The walls were adorned with vibrant artwork, and the room buzzed with conversations about business, ambitions, and weekend plans abroad. Aarav couldn't help but feel like an outsider, a visitor in Mahi's world.

"Welcome!" Mahi greeted him with her usual brightness, pulling him into the lively scene. "Come meet everyone!"

As the evening progressed, Mahi's friends asked Aarav questions about his work, his background, his ambitions. He answered politely, but each conversation felt like a test. Every answer he gave seemed to highlight how different he was from them. He could see Mahi's friends exchanging glances, as if measuring him against the standards of their fast-paced, metropolitan lives.

After some time, Mahi pulled out her phone and suggested, "Let's order some food! You have to try this amazing fusion restaurant I found."

Aarav hesitated. "Actually, I was hoping we could get something simpler. Maybe some local food?"

Mahi frowned slightly, her enthusiasm dimming. "Aarav, this is part of living in the city—you have to try new things! You can't keep holding on to the old ways."

The words hit him like a blow, and Aarav felt a knot form in his chest. "I'm not holding on to the past. I just don't want to lose the parts of myself that matter."

Mahi's face softened, but the tension was still there. "I'm not asking you to lose who you are. I just want you to experience everything this city has to offer. There's so much more out there."

Later that evening, despite Mahi's efforts to make him feel included, Aarav felt increasingly withdrawn. He felt like he was constantly being asked to prove himself, to show that he could fit into her world. The pressure was exhausting.

In the dim glow of their shared space, the weight of unspoken words had lingered between Aarav and Mahi for weeks. That night, after a particularly intense argument about their future, it finally spilled over.

Aarav couldn't hold back anymore. "Mahi," he began, his voice steady but filled with frustration, "I love you, but I can't keep pretending that this life is easy for me. I feel like I'm constantly being asked to change, to fit into a Mold that doesn't feel like me."

Mahi, taken aback, searched his face, her own expression softening from the fiery resolve she'd held onto during the argument. "I'm not trying to change you, Aarav," she replied, her voice a murmur. "I just want you to see your potential, to know you're capable of so much more. But maybe..." Her voice trailed off, and she looked away, blinking back the hurt that had pooled in her eyes. "Maybe I've been pushing too hard."

Aarav's heart softened as he saw the sadness behind her words. It wasn't about his potential, he realized, but the shared vision they had once dreamed of, a future that now seemed to pull them in two different directions. "It's not about my potential, Mahi. I just need space to be myself, to find a balance between the world I come from and the world you're asking me to build," he said, voice quieter, almost as if he were talking to himself.

Mahi looked at him, her gaze intense yet understanding. "I get it, Aarav. And I don't want to lose you over this. I never wanted to change who you are. Maybe... we've both been too focused on trying to make each other fit into our own ideas."

That night marked the beginning of a delicate truce, a gentle acknowledgment that they couldn't force each other into boxes. The honesty that had once seemed daunting now hung heavily in the air, illuminating the hidden crevices of their relationship. Their love couldn't survive if it meant erasing parts of themselves; instead, it would only flourish if they allowed each other the space to be fully themselves.

In the days that followed, they began to find a fragile balance. Aarav, despite his reluctance, made an effort to accompany Mahi to a few of her social gatherings and professional events. He stepped into her world, immersing himself tentatively in the bustling city life she thrived on. It felt overwhelming, yes, but he could see her beaming, watching him make an effort to understand what was important to her.

Mahi, in turn, let herself slow down, joining Aarav for quiet evenings in his favorite park or simply sharing a cup of chai in their apartment, with the city lights sparkling in the distance. She began to appreciate the quiet, introspective moments he cherished, moments that gave her a glimpse into the roots that had shaped him.

One evening, as they sat on a worn bench in the park, they watched the sun set in shades of orange and pink. Aarav took a deep breath, looking at the horizon. "I think I've been afraid," he confessed, his voice low. "Afraid that if I don't change, I'll lose you. But I'm starting to realize that maybe we don't have to choose between your world and mine."

Mahi turned to him; her eyes soft with understanding. "I never wanted you to lose yourself, Aarav. I just wanted you to see that there's room for both of us to grow. Together."

As they sat in the park, their fingers intertwined, a profound sense of peace settled over them. They realized that while their love had been forged through moments of passion and connection, it was their acceptance of each other's true selves that would sustain them.

With each passing day, they built upon this new understanding. Aarav continued to explore new experiences with Mahi, finding joy in the hustle and energy of the city in small doses, discovering that he could stretch himself without feeling as if he were breaking. For Mahi, it meant learning to slow down, to savor the quiet moments that Aarav treasured.

Their relationship was far from perfect; there were still moments of tension, small skirmishes when old insecurities surfaced, but each time, they returned to the commitment they had made to navigate these complexities together. They were two individuals with different backgrounds, but instead of letting their differences create a divide, they allowed them to be the foundation upon which they built something more enduring.

One late evening, with the quiet hum of street lamps illuminating their path, Aarav and Mahi strolled towards Aarav's neighbourhood. The familiar silence of the city at dusk seemed to wrap them in a cocoon, a shared space that, over the months, had become theirs. Aarav slowed his pace, glancing over at Mahi. There was a softness in his gaze that hadn't been there before—a warmth that had grown through countless conversations, laughter, and moments of silent support. As he walked beside her, he felt a new sense of calm, like he was letting go of something heavy.

"You know, Mahi," Aarav began, his voice tender, "I'm realizing that embracing parts of your world doesn't mean I have to abandon my own. I've always been scared of that, afraid that if I leaned too far into your life, I'd lose my footing in mine. But now...I see that our worlds can coexist. They don't have to clash; they can actually complement each other."

Mahi listened, her heart swelling at his words. She felt her own sense of understanding settle deeper, a sense that her life didn't have to overwhelm his. She could tell that Aarav was opening up to possibilities—possibilities where they could grow together, without losing themselves.

A smile spread across her face, and she turned to him with a spark of excitement. "Aarav, let's go for dinner," she suggested. "There's this amazing place I want to take you to—*Naushijaan*. It's famous for its large range of Awadhi kebabs and Mughlai dishes."

Aarav chuckled softly. "*Naushijaan?* Isn't that the one near your place?"

"Exactly!" Mahi laughed. "And trust me, it's one of the finest. It'll give you a real taste of Lucknow's heritage."

Aarav looked at her, a small smile playing on his lips. It had become a familiar ritual—Aarav would walk her home every evening, catching a public bus back afterward. She'd often urged him to buy a scooter, teasing him for taking the trouble of using public transport just to be with her on these walks. But each time, Aarav would brush it off with a shy smile, saying it wasn't something he could afford right now.

"Why don't you just get a two-wheeler, Aarav?" Mahi asked again, nudging him. "I mean, you don't have to keep taking the bus because of me."

He looked down, nodding with a gentle smile. "We'll talk about it later. For now, you know I don't eat non-veg," he reminded her gently, hoping she wouldn't feel disappointed.

"Oh, come on!" she nudged him playfully, her eyes sparkling. "*Naushijaan has more than just Mughlai.* They have coffee and snacks too, and I really want you to try it out. Besides, I'd love to have some photos for memories!"

Despite his reluctance, Aarav found himself agreeing, simply because he knew it mattered to her.

She had a way of making things brighter, more inviting, and he wanted to share this part of her world, even if it was outside his comfort zone. With her hand gently tugging his, they soon found themselves at the dimly lit, rustic restaurant, the scent of spices and roasted meat filling the air. The decor was lavish, with intricately carved wooden arches and rich tapestries, immersing them in a world that felt timeless and indulgent.

They ordered coffee and a few light snacks, much to Aarav's relief, while Mahi eagerly pointed out the dishes around them. "See, that's the signature Awadhi kebab. And look at that biryani! The flavors here are so unique," she explained with excitement.

As they sipped their coffee, Mahi looked at Aarav, her eyes filled with gratitude. "Thank you, Aarav, for coming here with me," she said softly. "I know it's not your style, but...it means a lot to me."

Aarav reached out, gently squeezing her hand, and smiled back. "Seeing you happy is more important to me than any meal preference. And you know...maybe I'll even surprise you and try the biryani next time."

She laughed, the sound carrying warmth and affection, and leaned a little closer to him. There was something unspoken between them, a connection that didn't need words, filling the silence with a gentle understanding. Their hands remained intertwined, and in that moment, Aarav realized that they didn't need to say everything aloud; some things were felt more deeply when left unsaid.

The night air was cool as they left the restaurant, strolling back through quiet streets. Mahi felt a certain tenderness from Aarav, one that was new but deeply comforting. She gently leaned her head on his shoulder, letting herself sink into the moment. For once, Aarav didn't pull back or tense up. He let her rest against him, feeling that this, right here, was where he wanted to be.

As they walked, Mahi began speaking about her dreams, her love for the culture and vibrancy of the city, and her desire to share it all with him. She'd always been more expressive, more open to blending experiences, while Aarav often stayed reserved, cautious of exposing his vulnerabilities. Yet here, under the quiet sky, he found himself sharing pieces of his own dreams—dreams he had tucked away, believing they would fade over time.

"I've always thought my path was too set, too strict," Aarav admitted, his voice soft. "But you make me believe that maybe I can still take risks, open up a bit, and have more than just one life."

Mahi listened, her heart aching with love and pride for this man who was willing to let down his walls, if only a little. She turned to him, brushing a gentle hand along his cheek. "Aarav, you don't have to change who you are for me. All I want is for you to be happy, however that looks for you."

Her words were filled with a sincerity that reached into the depths of him. He pulled her into a tender embrace, their bodies wrapped in a warmth that went beyond the night's chill. Holding her close, he realized that maybe, just maybe, he could allow himself to dream a little differently.

As they continued walking in silence, it was a silence no longer heavy with tension, no longer weighed down by unsaid things. It was a peaceful, shared quiet—filled with the understanding that they were two different people with unique dreams, yet they could walk this path together, enriching each other's lives.

When they reached Mahi's home, Aarav hesitated. The moment felt too precious to end, and he was reluctant to let it go. They lingered, their fingers intertwined, eyes locked in a gaze that held a depth word couldn't capture.

"Goodnight, Aarav," Mahi whispered, her voice warm and affectionate.

"Goodnight, Mahi," he replied softly, brushing a gentle kiss on her forehead—a gesture that spoke volumes of the affection growing between them.

As he walked back home, Aarav felt a quiet joy filling him. He no longer felt the nagging fear of losing himself in someone else's world. Instead, he felt a new strength, a certainty that he could build a life that embraced both his dreams and hers. And with that thought, he knew that they could face whatever challenges lay ahead, hand in hand, their unique worlds no longer clashing, but blending into something beautiful.

In the following weeks, this balance became easier to maintain. Aarav, despite his initial resistance, allowed himself to be vulnerable, discovering that Mahi's support didn't require him to be perfect. Meanwhile, Mahi learned to appreciate the moments of stillness that Aarav offered, moments that reminded her there was beauty in slowing down, in letting things simply be.

Their journey together was like a slow dance, with each step bringing them closer, teaching them that love could thrive not despite their differences but because of them.

Part 3: Perspective Shifts

Chapter 6: Unwritten Emotions

As they spend more time together, unspoken feelings start to develop. However, neither is willing to admit it due to their "contractual" relationship and fear of emotional vulnerability.

As the weeks rolled into months, the bond between Aarav and Mahi deepened, yet it was shrouded in layers of unspoken feelings. Every laugh shared, every late-night conversation, only served to amplify the emotions simmering just beneath the surface. Yet, both were ensnared by their "contractual" relationship—a tenuous arrangement that both defined and confined them. The fear of emotional vulnerability loomed large, creating an invisible barrier between their hearts.

"Aarav, I don't want to be stuck in these part-time jobs forever," she said, her words hanging in the silence of the night. "I want to be more. I want to make a real difference." There was a tremor of hope in her voice, the kind of vulnerability that only someone like Aarav could understand.

Aarav listened quietly, the familiar comfort of her voice blending with the stillness around him. He could feel the weight of her words, the silent longing beneath them. He had always seen this fire in Mahi—the quiet strength she carried, the hunger for something more.

"Mahi, for now, just sleep," Aarav said gently, his voice warm and reassuring, like a soft caress over the phone. "It's already past midnight. We'll meet tomorrow at the same café where we met last time, and then we'll talk about everything." He paused, letting his words sink in. "There's no need to think so much tonight."

A soft sigh escaped Mahi's lips, her tension easing under his calm tone. She trusted him, the way his words always felt like an anchor when her thoughts began to drift. The next day, as the golden hues of the late afternoon sun began to fade, they met at their favorite café—the place that had become their quiet retreat, a haven for their shared moments. The dimly lit café buzzed with the usual hum of conversation, but for Mahi and Aarav, the world had shrunk to just the two of them. Their regular meetings had become a routine, a refuge from the pressures of exams and future uncertainties. Sitting across from each other, time seemed to lose its hold, and for a moment, everything felt effortless.

But Mahi's expression, once glowing with excitement over her studies, now carried the weight of hesitation. She looked up from her tea, her fingers tracing the rim of the cup.

Mahi took a deep breath, her gaze steady as she met Aarav's eyes across the table. There was a quiet resolve in her voice, a sense of clarity she hadn't expressed before.

"I've made up my mind, Aarav," she said softly. "I want to do an MBA, just like you suggested. I think it's time I take that step."

Aarav felt a warmth spread through him as he listened, his heart swelling with pride and affection. He had always believed in Mahi's potential, and hearing her say those words filled him with quiet joy. He smiled, a mix of encouragement and care in his expression.

"That's amazing, Mahi," he said, his voice gentle yet full of support. "You've made the right decision."

Aarav leaned in slightly, his tone becoming more practical, yet still filled with affection. "Now that you've made your decision, I think you should join some CAT coaching," he said, his voice soft but firm. "It will give you a proper structure and help you stay focused. You'll ace it. Just leave the job for some time and focus on your studies."

But Mahi's smile faltered, her fingers tightening around the cup, as if holding onto something fragile. She looked away, her voice shrinking in a way that betrayed the inner struggle she always kept hidden.

"Aarav," she murmured, her voice small and almost defeated. "I can't afford coaching."

Aarav's brows furrowed, concern flooding his eyes as she continued. "My family... they need me to keep this job. There's no way I can just stop working and start preparing for an MBA. I can't let them down. They rely on me." Aarav's heart tightened at the vulnerability in her eyes. He could feel the mix of frustration and determination building inside him. How could she give up so easily when she was capable of so much more? "Mahi," he said, his voice firm but gentle, "don't worry about the fees. I'll help you. Just focus on your studies, on your dream. We'll figure out the rest."

"Mahi, listen to me," he said, his voice gentle but firm, his gaze unwavering as he looked into her eyes. "You've always done everything for everyone else, and I know how much your family means to you. But this—this is your dream. You deserve to give it a real chance.

Her eyes widened, surprise flickering across her face, followed by something softer—gratitude, maybe even disbelief. "You really think I can do it?"

Aarav reached across the table, his hand brushing hers. "Absolutely," he said, the intensity of his belief washing over her like a tidal wave. "Just give it everything you've got. I believe in you, Mahi." In that moment, the weight on Mahi's heart seemed to lighten, just a little. She wasn't alone in this anymore. The dream that had once felt so distant now seemed within reach, as long as he was there beside her. And for the first time in a long time, hope flickered in her chest, fragile but real.

They sat there in silence, their hands still entwined on the table, the café around them fading into the background. It wasn't just a promise of love—it was a shared belief, a quiet assurance that together, they could conquer the uncertainties that lay ahead.

From that day, everything changed. Mahi enrolled in the coaching program, and the two of them fell into a new rhythm—meeting every day after her classes, whether at Aarav's place or in a cozy corner of the same café. Time passed like sand slipping through their fingers, but with each meeting, the bond between them grew stronger, the conversations deeper, the silence more comfortable. They laughed, studied, dreamed, and without realizing it, they had started to enjoy each other's company far more than they had anticipated.

While Mahi buried herself in her CAT prep, Aarav quietly began his own journey toward the UPSC exam. They both had goals, dreams that danced on distant horizons, and yet every moment spent together felt like a beautiful pause, as if time was only measured by the heartbeats they shared.

The bittersweet reality lingered, but Mahi's ambitions didn't stop there. Despite missing the CAT deadlines, Aarav encouraged her to aim for the MAT exam, assuring her that it was another step toward her MBA dream. And she trusted him—she always had. With relentless dedication, she threw herself into the MAT, and when the results came in, she had achieved the impossible—99.99 percentile.

But Aarav's victory wasn't far behind. The UPSC Preliminary had been a challenge, yet he cleared it on his first attempt. The thrill of success surged through them both, but it also meant decisions needed to be made, paths had to be chosen.

Together, they began scouring universities for Mahi's MBA, looking for options that could offer her a future without burdening her family. Aarav had already made up his mind—he wanted her to apply to the university where he had pursued his MBA in international business, a place that granted full scholarships to top-performing students. Mahi wouldn't have to pay a single rupee. It was perfect, except for one thing—her family wasn't convinced. The university was far, too distant for comfort, and her parents and brother weren't willing to let her go that easily.

Aarav stood by her side through every difficult conversation, every plea, every negotiation. He could see the fire in her eyes, the determination to make this dream happen. And after what felt like endless back-and-forth, her family finally relented. Mahi had won, not just the battle for her education but the right to carve out her own path.

As the months flew by, Mahi's hard work paid off. The day she received her acceptance letter to a private university in Punjab was filled with elation—but also a quiet sadness that clung to the edges of her joy. "I got in," she whispered, holding the letter as though it were a fragile thing. Aarav, standing beside her, smiled with pride, but his heart ached. The future was calling, and it would take her far away from Lucknow, far away from Aarav. The reality settled in like a slow burn.

"You'll do amazing things there," Aarav said one evening as they sat under the stars, the weight of the moment heavy between them.

Mahi looked at him, her heart swelling with emotion she wasn't sure she could contain. "I wouldn't have made it without you, Aarav."

He shook his head. "You were always going to make it, Mahi. I just reminded you of what you were capable of."

The distance between them felt sharper now, but in that moment, with the night wrapping around them like a warm embrace, they both knew that whatever came next—whatever dreams they chased, no matter how far apart they would be—their connection, their story, would always be intertwined, written in the spaces between words left unspoken.

He was proud of her achievement but also deeply anxious about the distance that would come between them. "You're going to thrive there, Mahi. But what about us? What will this mean for our partnership?" he asked, his voice betraying his unease.

As Mahi prepared to leave for college, the air was thick with a sense of anticipation, excitement, and an undercurrent of bittersweet emotions. She was leaving Lucknow, a place filled with memories, comfort, and familiarity, to start a new chapter of her life at a university in Punjab. It wasn't just about moving to a new city; it was about stepping into the unknown, embracing independence, and exploring her potential. But with every new beginning comes an inevitable end to what was, and that tugged at Aarav's heart like nothing else.

Aarav had been by her side throughout the days leading up to her departure. They spent hours shopping, making sure she had everything she needed for her studies and daily life. From clothes to essentials, from stationery to the little trinkets that would make her hostel room feel like home. Aarav, ever the planner, took care of it all so that Mahi wouldn't have to struggle or feel alone in a new city. His eyes meticulously scanned the aisles, his hands picking up every item he thought might bring her a touch of comfort, ensuring she would never feel the absence of familiarity in her new surroundings.

But there was one gift that stood out above all else—the books. Aarav had spent years accumulating these MBA books, each one carefully chosen, underlined, and worn from use. They were more than just textbooks; they were part of his journey, his memories, his growth. And now, he handed them over to Mahi, as if entrusting her with a piece of his soul. Each book he passed on came with a handwritten message, something personal and intimate scribbled inside the covers—words of encouragement, love, and hope. Messages like, *"Whenever you feel overwhelmed, remember I'm with you, just a page away,"* or *"This book helped me through the toughest times, and now it's here to help you."*

For Aarav, these messages were more than just notes—they were anchors to keep them connected. He wanted Mahi to feel his presence every time she opened a book, a silent reminder that no matter the distance, he was always there with her. Each word, written late into the night, was filled with love, longing, and a deep need to protect her in any way he could.

As Mahi packed her bags, Aarav wrestled with an intense sense of possessiveness. He wanted to be her protector, her anchor in this sea of change. Though he trusted her with all his heart, the idea of her being in a new city without him left him unsettled. He tried not to let it show, but it manifested in little ways—like double-checking her packing, insisting on buying extra things she didn't even think she needed, or reminding her to call him every night. There was a vulnerability in him, a fear that this new chapter in her life might somehow drift them apart, even if he knew Mahi would never let that happen.

One evening, as they sat together surrounded by packed bags, Aarav couldn't hold back his thoughts anymore.

"It's everything you worked for," he said, his voice soft but edged with something unsaid. He was proud of her, more than he could ever express, but the thought of her leaving Lucknow, of leaving him behind, left an unspoken void between them.

Mahi could sense his unease, the way his hand held hers a little tighter, the way his eyes lingered on her face as if trying to memorize every detail. She smiled gently, leaning into his shoulder.

"I'll always be loyal to you, Aarav. This doesn't change how I feel about our connection," she reassured him, though a hint of uncertainty lingered in her own eyes. She knew this distance would be hard, not just for him but for her too. But she believed in them, in the strength of what they shared.

Finally, the day of departure arrived. Mahi's tickets were booked, and her family, along with Aarav, accompanied her to Lucknow station. The platform was buzzing with the usual hustle and bustle, but for them, time seemed to slow down. Every moment felt precious, every word spoken felt heavy with meaning. They were running out of time, and yet, miraculously, the train was delayed by two hours, giving them a little more time together.

Mahi, Aarav, and her family found a spot in the first-class AC waiting room, where they settled in, trying to make the most of their extra time. They talked, laughed, and reminisced about old times, but there was an undercurrent of sadness in the air—one that couldn't be ignored. The thought of saying goodbye was looming, and neither Mahi nor Aarav knew how to prepare for it.

As they sat side by side, Mahi, in her usual playful manner, looked at Aarav and nudged him lightly. "You know, you're such a good storyteller. You write so well," she said, her eyes twinkling with mischief. "You should write our story someday."

Aarav chuckled, but there was a seriousness in his eyes. He looked at her for a moment, taking in her words. The idea of immortalizing their journey, of writing down every moment they had shared, touched something deep inside him. He nodded, smiling softly. "I will. I'll write our story," he promised, the weight of the commitment settling in his heart.

Mahi's eyes softened at his words, and for a brief moment, the impending separation seemed to fade away. "Promise me you will," she whispered, her voice barely audible above the noise of the station.

"I promise," Aarav replied, his voice firm, filled with the conviction of a man who knew that some stories were meant to be told.

The two hours flew by faster than they expected, and before they knew it, the train had arrived. The time had come for Mahi to leave, and Aarav's heart clenched at the sight of her walking toward the platform, her bags in tow. He walked alongside her, his hand never leaving hers until the very last moment.

As the train began to pull away, Aarav stood there, watching her through the window, a thousand emotions swirling in his chest. He waved, trying to hold back the tears, but the ache in his heart was undeniable.

And as the train carried Mahi away, he made a silent vow to himself—to write their story, not just for her, but for both of them. Because even though the distance separated them, their love, their connection, was something that could never be erased.

In that moment, Aarav knew that their story was only just beginning.

And Mahi last words while leaving to Lucknow....

"I'll always be loyal to you, Aarav. This doesn't change how I feel about our connection," she reassured him, though a hint of uncertainty lingered in her eyes.

"It's everything you worked for," he said, though the thought of her leaving Lucknow, of leaving him, left an unspoken void between them.

In a tale woven with long-distance yearning, emotional turbulence, and deep-rooted love, Mahi and Aarav find themselves caught between their personal aspirations and the bond they share. Their love, once seamless and carefree, slowly begins to evolve as the physical distance between them brings forth insecurities, possessiveness, and growth in unexpected ways.

Mahi had always been a free spirit, eager to explore new horizons, and when the opportunity came for her to attend university in Punjab, it felt like the beginning of a new chapter in her life. On the other hand, Aarav, staying back in Lucknow to prepare for his UPSC main exams with his airline job, grappled with a sense of unease. The thought of Mahi living a life independent of him was both exhilarating and frightening. As Mahi adjusted to the new academic environment, different from anything she had ever known, she often sought Aarav's help. Despite the newness of her surroundings, she remained deeply connected to him.

In the early days of their relationship, the distance between Mahi and Aarav had been nothing more than a minor inconvenience, a test of their resilience that they both seemed willing to conquer. Their daily messages were like small beacons of affection, lighting up their days in ways they hadn't imagined possible. Each call, whether brief or leisurely, was a gentle reminder that they weren't alone on this journey. They shared every moment they could – Aarav would recount long hours buried in books, sharing the mental strain of studying for the UPSC, while Mahi would talk about her bustling college life, filled with new faces, professors, and experiences that she was eager to dive into.

But as Mahi began to find herself immersed in college life; Aarav's possessiveness started to slip through the cracks in his steady, calm demeanor. UPSC was approaching quickly, with the date set for October 5th, 2012 to October 26th, and as it loomed closer, Aarav's focus sharpened to an almost single-minded intensity. His days were filled with relentless hours of reading, testing, and strategizing. To Aarav, passing the UPSC was more than just a test; it was a lifeline, a way out of the struggles that had defined his life for so long. Yet, with Mahi's college life bustling and full of new experiences, Aarav's dedication began to breed insecurity.

One evening, after a day of exhaustive studies, Aarav received a message from Mahi: "Hey Aarav! Guess what? The girls in my class and I are planning to go out tomorrow night. There's this new café everyone's been raving about – I can't wait to check it out!"

Aarav's heart tightened. As he read the message, an uneasy feeling stirred within him, a hint of possessiveness he couldn't quite suppress. He messaged back after a moment, choosing his words carefully but unable to shake the jealous thoughts that had begun to creep in. "Are you sure you want to go out with your new friends from university?" he typed, aware that he sounded far more insecure than he intended. His fingers hovered over the screen before he pressed send. A few moments later, he added another message, "You'll be meeting new people, and I just... I don't want you to forget about us, Mahi."

Mahi's reply came quickly, tinged with a patient gentleness that she always used whenever Aarav's insecurities threatened to pull him under. "Aarav, of course I won't forget about us. You don't have to worry about that." She paused, then added reassuringly, "You know that I believe in you and want you to stay focused on your exam right now. I know how much UPSC means to you – it's your dream, and I'm here to support you in every way."

Reading her message, Aarav felt a swell of affection but also a quiet pang of guilt. He knew that Mahi understood the weight of his ambitions, knew how hard he had worked to make this dream a reality. And though he wanted to be nothing but happy for her as she made friends and explored this new phase of her life, part of him felt left behind, trapped within the walls of his own room, surrounded by piles of notes and textbooks.

Later that night, Mahi called him, her voice as soothing as the soft hum of a lullaby. "Aarav," she murmured gently, "You're the one who always told me to go after what makes me happy. I want the same for you. Right now, that's your UPSC preparation. We don't have to talk every single day if that's what's stressing you out. I'll always be here, whether it's through texts or calls or when we can't talk at all. Just don't let this come between us."

Aarav sighed, comforted by her words. "You're right, Mahi. I know you are. I just... It's hard sometimes. Knowing that you're out there, meeting new people, living your life, while I'm stuck here with my books and deadlines."

Her soft laughter filtered through the phone, warm and full of understanding. "You're not 'stuck,' Aarav. You're working toward something amazing. And I'm right here, cheering for you. I'll be here after every exam, every study session, waiting to hear from you, just as I always have."

In that moment, Aarav realized how lucky he was to have someone who saw through his fears and understood his dreams so intimately. He promised himself he would work harder, stay focused, and let Mahi have her space without allowing his insecurities to tarnish their relationship.

The next day, as Mahi went out with her new friends, Aarav poured himself into his studies with renewed vigor. He told himself that he was fighting not just for himself, but for both of them, for the future they had dreamt of sharing. He read until his eyes burned, underlining key points, testing himself on the material, and visualizing the day when he would finally achieve his goals.

For the next few weeks, their conversations became less frequent but more meaningful. Mahi would send him thoughtful messages, little reminders of her support that warmed his heart. She told him about her classes and friends, about the professors who inspired her, and the new ambitions she was discovering for herself. And though a part of Aarav missed the easy, uninterrupted attention she had once given him, he reminded himself that this was what it meant to grow - for both of them to pursue their dreams and trust that their bond would only grow stronger with time.

But one evening, as Aarav scrolled through social media during a brief study break, he stumbled upon a picture of Mahi with her friends at a recent college event. She looked radiant, her laughter captured in a candid moment that made her look both beautiful and distant, as if she was slipping further away from him with each passing day. A pang of jealousy flared in his chest, fierce and unwelcome, and he closed the app, unable to shake the feeling.

When they spoke later that night, Aarav's frustration slipped through in his tone. "I saw the picture from your college event," he said, trying to keep his voice light. "Looks like you're having a lot of fun without me."

Mahi sensed the tension and sighed, a gentle understanding softening her voice. "Aarav, it's just a college event. You know I would've loved to have you there, but... I'm here, and you're there. We're both working toward something important. This is just part of it."

"I know, I know," Aarav mumbled, feeling foolish and a little ashamed. "It's just... hard sometimes. I miss you."

Mahi's voice softened. "I miss you too, Aarav. But I need you to trust me, just like I trust you. There are people here, yes, but they don't hold a candle to what we have. You and I are building something bigger than all of this. Can we hold onto that?"

Her words soothed him, melting the sharp edge of his jealousy, leaving only the warmth of her steady faith in him. He promised her then that he would keep his focus on his exam, and let her enjoy this new chapter in her life, free from the weight of his insecurities. He would trust her, just as she trusted him.

The UPSC mains drew closer, and Aarav could feel the tension building as each day passed. Mahi sent him small messages every morning, little notes of encouragement that steadied him whenever he felt overwhelmed. Her words were like an invisible hand holding his, grounding him even when she was miles away. And when he finally sat down to take the exam, he felt as if she were right there beside him, her presence wrapping around him like a warm blanket.

When the exams were finally over, Aarav called Mahi, his voice a mix of exhaustion and elation. "I did it," he whispered, relief and pride evident in his tone. "I gave it everything I had, Mahi."

Her voice bubbled over with joy. "I never doubted you, not for a single moment! I'm so proud of you, Aarav. Now, you can finally breathe and relax a little. You've worked so hard – you deserve this moment."

In the days that followed, their conversations returned to the easy, affectionate rhythm they had once shared. They talked about their dreams and the future they both envisioned, a life built on the strength of their love and the resilience they had nurtured in the face of every obstacle. They shared the details of each day, the small victories and setbacks, finding comfort in the knowledge that they had survived yet another test.

And as they looked to the future, Aarav realized that the love they shared was no longer bound by the uncertainty of distance or the pressures of ambition. It was a love that had been tempered and strengthened by the trials they had faced, a love that had grown deeper with every struggle and sacrifice. For in their time apart, they had learned that true love was not about possession or control, but about trust, faith, and the quiet strength to let each other grow.

His insecurities startled Mahi. She paused, processing his reaction. "Aarav, I'm not going to forget you. But I need to experience this. It's important for my growth," she responded gently, but a flicker of irritation rose within her.

"I know," Aarav said, his brow furrowed. "It's just hard for me to accept that you'll be out there, alone. You might change. You might... meet someone else."

The tension between them became palpable, Mahi's frustration mixing with Aarav's possessiveness. Although she never openly confronted Aarav, his words began to weigh on her mind, creating an undercurrent of anxiety. She worried that his insecurity might stifle her independence and her need to explore this new chapter in her life. Despite this, their bond persisted, even as it felt strained.

As the first semester came to a close, Mahi thrived. She made new friends, embraced her independence, and excelled in her studies, achieving impressive grades. However, with each new success, a pang of guilt tugged at her heart. She knew that while she was growing, Aarav's insecurities were festering back in Lucknow. He missed her deeply and, despite encouraging her to pursue her dreams, felt as if he was losing her to this new life.

Back in Lucknow, Aarav found himself scrolling through her social media posts, anxious to catch a glimpse of how she was adapting to her new world. Every post, every update reminded him of the distance that separated them, making him feel increasingly like an outsider in her life. One evening, unable to shake his worries, he texted her, hoping for reassurance. "Hey, Mahi. How's everything going? Are you settling in?"

Her reply came quickly, brimming with enthusiasm. "It's great! I love the campus and my classes. I'm making new friends, too!"

Aarav's heart sank slightly. He wanted to be happy for her, but every word reinforced the widening gap between them. "That's awesome! Just remember, I'm still here for you," he typed, feeling a gnawing sense of insecurity.

Mahi, sensing the weight behind his words, reassured him, "Of course, Aarav. You mean a lot to me. But I also need to figure out who I am here."

Her response, though kind, echoed a truth that both of them were reluctant to face. Mahi was discovering her identity, growing into herself, and Aarav feared that he was becoming less a part of her new life. His possessiveness, once a reflection of his deep love for her, now began to feel like a barrier to her freedom.

As Mahi flourished in Punjab, enjoying the vibrant student life, each new social event or study session brought a pang of anxiety about Aarav's reaction. After one particularly fun outing with her friends, she received a call from Aarav. His voice, warm as always, carried a hint of something she couldn't quite place. "I hope you're not forgetting about me in all this excitement," he said softly, his words steeped in insecurity.

Mahi's heart ached. "Of course not, Aarav. You're always on my mind. But I'm just trying to adjust to everything here."

Their conversations became more strained, each word careful and deliberate. Mahi could feel Aarav's possessiveness intensifying, and it began to suffocate her. She longed for his support in this new phase of her life, but the weight of his expectations felt like chains holding her back. Mahi would often call Aarav, her voice tinged with a mix of playfulness and longing, asking him to visit her in Punjab. She had been living there for a while now, and the distance between them had begun to feel more palpable with each passing day. "You know, Aarav, every weekend my friends make plans to go out, and I'm the only one left behind in the hostel, talking to you on the phone. Most of the girls here are in relationships—they go out with their boyfriends, and I'm stuck here feeling alone," she'd say, her words carrying a subtle undertone of disappointment.

Her frustration wasn't just about the loneliness; it was the growing feeling that, despite being in a relationship, she was still missing out on the companionship others seemed to enjoy. She wanted to spend time with Aarav, to feel close to him again, especially when everyone around her seemed to have someone by their side. "It's not that I don't like talking to you," she would clarify, her tone softening, "but it's hard when everyone else is out having fun, and I'm just here."

Aarav understood her feelings. He knew she craved the warmth of his presence, the joy of shared moments that could ease the distance between them. But he was caught in a whirlwind of responsibilities—his full-time job, long shifts at the airline, and the relentless preparation for his UPSC Mains. Every day felt like a battle against time, with little space left for anything beyond his ambitions. He wanted to visit her, to be there for her, but his life had become a delicate balancing act between dreams and reality.

Whenever Mahi asked him to come to Punjab, Aarav would feel a pang of guilt, knowing he couldn't fulfil her request. "I really want to come, Mahi, but I'm swamped right now with work and the UPSC prep. I promise, as soon as things settle down, I'll make it a point to visit," he would say, trying to reassure her, though deep down he knew how much his absence was affecting her.

There were times when Mahi's disappointment was harder to hide. Her calls would become less playful, the lightness in her voice replaced by a quiet sadness. "You always say you'll come, but you never do," she would say softly, trying not to sound accusatory, though Aarav could sense the hurt behind her words. "Whenever I call, I hope maybe this time you'll say you're coming, but it never happens."

Aarav would fall silent on the other end of the line, torn between his responsibilities and the love he felt for her. He wanted nothing more than to drop everything and be by her side, to ease the loneliness she was feeling. But his hands were tied, and every time he tried to explain, he felt like he was failing her. "I know it's hard, Mahi," he would whisper, wishing he could reach through the phone and make everything right. "But this is just for a little while longer. Once the exams are over, I'll make up for it, I promise."

But Mahi's patience was wearing thin. Despite understanding his struggles, the distance weighed heavily on her heart. She wanted more than just promises over the phone. She wanted to see him, to spend time with him in person, to feel that he was as invested in their relationship as she was.

Some evenings, after another failed attempt to get Aarav to visit, Mahi would sit in her hostel room, staring at her phone, her thoughts tangled in frustration and longing. It wasn't that she didn't understand Aarav's situation—she knew how hard he was working—but the distance made everything harder. She missed him deeply, and as the weeks turned into months, the separation became more than just physical; it started to feel like an emotional chasm.

And yet, despite her disappointment, she held on to hope. She believed that once Aarav's exam was over, they would find their way back to each other—stronger, more connected, and ready to bridge the distance that had been keeping them apart. Until then, all she could do was wait, hoping that the love they shared would be enough to carry them through the moments of loneliness and unspoken heartache.

Then, one fine day, Aarav decided to surprise her. He booked a train to Jalandhar, Punjab, determined to close the distance, even if only for a short while. When Mahi called him that evening, he was already at the train station, but he didn't want to spoil the surprise. "I'm just heading to my hometown," he told her, his voice muffled by the noise of the station.

Confused, Mahi asked, "Why didn't you tell me about this sudden trip?"

Aarav, eager to maintain the surprise, quickly ended the call. The next day, he arrived in her city and checked into a hotel near her university. After freshening up, he made his way to the campus, using his status as an alumnus to gain access. Standing in front of her hostel, Aarav felt a rush of nervous excitement as he called her.

Mahi didn't answer at first, and when she finally called him back, she apologized, "Sorry, Aarav, I couldn't take your call. I was in the shower."

In a soft voice, Aarav asked, "Where are you right now?"

"I'm just in the hostel, heading to get some breakfast. I missed the mess breakfast," she said, unaware of what was about to unfold.

"Can we have breakfast together today?" Aarav asked, his tone filled with anticipation.

Mahi, caught off guard, replied, "What? What do you mean?"

Aarav smiled to himself. "Just look outside your window."

When Mahi peered out, she saw Aarav standing there in the blue t-shirt she had gifted him. Tears welled up in her eyes as she shouted his name, "Aarav! Aarav!" before running to meet him. As she reached him, they embraced tightly, the months of distance dissolving in that one moment. For the first time in four months, they were together.

Aarav looked at her with a smile, "What do you want to eat?"

Mahi, still overwhelmed with happiness, replied, "Anything, as long as I'm with you."

After applying for a night-out leave from the hostel, they spent the day exploring the city, sharing her favorite meals, shopping, and talking like they used to. Mahi even bought Aarav a watch as a gift, a token of her love and a celebration of her academic success.

That day felt like a dream. Mahi couldn't believe that Aarav was really there with her, after all the emotional highs and lows they had endured. The hours flew by, and despite spending an entire day together, Mahi felt as if it wasn't enough. They returned to Aarav's hotel for the night, relishing in the closeness they had missed for so long.

As they sat quietly in the dim light of the hotel room, the air between them thick with unspoken thoughts, Mahi broke the silence. She turned to him, her eyes a mixture of excitement and warmth. "Hey, Aarav," she asked softly, her voice carrying a gentle curiosity, "your UPSC result is coming out this Friday, right?"

Aarav gave a slight nod, his expression tense, a small frown forming as he looked away, his gaze settling somewhere on the floor. "Yeah," he replied, his voice barely above a whisper. "That's actually why I came down here. I needed to be somewhere familiar... somewhere that feels safe." He took a long, deep breath, and for a moment, his composure seemed to slip. "Honestly, Mahi, I'm nervous. I keep thinking... what if I don't make it?"

Mahi paused, her gaze softening as she searched his face, sensing the weight of his worry. Slowly, she placed a reassuring hand on his arm. "Aarav, you've put everything you have into this," she said with a quiet, steady confidence. "You're stronger than you know. No matter what happens, I'm right here. This is just one part of the journey. You've already come so far."

As they sat together, words flowing softly between them, the night drifted by, unnoticed, like a gentle breeze. In the quiet closeness, every worry faded, and time seemed to pause, holding them in a tender, unspoken promise. The hours melted away, and with each passing moment, Aarav found himself feeling lighter, as if just her presence had softened the edges of his fears. But the next morning came too quickly.

Aarav had to return to Lucknow for his office, and Mahi to her hostel. As they parted at the train station, they both knew that while the distance between them had physically lessened for a moment, the emotional journey they were on was far from over.

And yet, despite the challenges, their love remained – complex, evolving, but always present.

"UPSC mains results day 22 March 2013"

And finally, the day arrived. For the world, it was just another ordinary morning, the sun rising as it always did, casting its golden light across the city. But for Aarav and Mahi, this morning held a weight that only they could feel—a fragile blend of hope,fear, and dreams hanging in the balance. Each second seemed to echo with possibilities, every tick of the clock carrying them closer to an answer that would either lift them or bring them crashing down. Together, they sat in silence, feeling the quiet hum of anticipation, knowing that by day's end, their world could look entirely different.

Aarav left for the office that morning, trying to carry on as if it were just another day, but the wait gnawed at him. Mahi, unable to sit still, called him repeatedly, her voice bright with encouragement yet laced with her own quiet worry. As the afternoon crept by, Aarav finally received a notification—*the results were out.* His heart pounded as he reached for his admit card, hands trembling slightly as he began typing in his roll number. On the other end of the line, Mahi listened intently, each tap of the keyboard sending her heart racing.

"What happened?" she whispered anxiously, barely able to hold her breath.

A few seconds later, a heavy silence fell between them. Aarav's voice came through, low and filled with disbelief. "I didn't qualify, Mahi. I... I failed." And before she could respond, he hung up, needing a moment to let it sink in.

The hours that followed were a blur. His mind felt numb, echoing with shattered hopes. His phone rang incessantly—Mahi, his parents, friends—all wanting to know, all waiting for the answer he dreaded to speak aloud. But he couldn't bring himself to answer. Only late that night, under the weight of exhaustion, did he finally return the calls, his voice a mix of acceptance and quiet sorrow as he spoke to his family and, finally, to Mahi.

Aarav's journey to the UPSC mains was one fueled by long nights, endless hours of preparation, and a deep-rooted desire to bring stability and pride to his family. But the exam he had poured himself into did not yield the outcome he had hoped for. In 2012, with the daunting requirement of two optional subjects, he chose management—a familiar domain—and economics, which, while interesting, was entirely new to him. He found himself struggling to master the economic theories, nuances, and vast syllabus within the time constraints. Despite his relentless effort, he couldn't cover it all, and when the results were announced, he discovered that he hadn't made it through the mains. His dreams of clearing UPSC in his first attempt were dashed, and with them, the hope he had nurtured so carefully.

The weight of failure was heavy. Aarav had built so much around this attempt—his family's dreams, his future plans, and his own self-worth. His family, too, had poured in support, encouraging him through every high and low, and now, as he struggled to comprehend the outcome, their disappointment mirrored his own. For a while, he found himself trapped in silence, needing time to let the reality settle in.

Amidst this somber period, Mahi was a constant presence, her words weaving strength into his wounded resolve. She refused to let him be swallowed by defeat. Each conversation was a reminder that he had come closer than many ever had. "You cleared UPSC prelims on your first try, Aarav. That's no small achievement," she would remind him, her voice steady yet gentle. "This is UPSC; it demands patience and time. Don't be upset; think about your next attempt." Her encouragement was unwavering, her belief in his ability stronger than his doubts. She pushed him to see beyond his loss, to acknowledge his accomplishments and prepare himself to face the challenge again.

But despite her optimism, Aarav knew he needed a moment to grieve the loss, to fully digest this failure before he could gather the strength to start over. Yet, even in his lowest moments, Mahi's words lingered. She had lit a small flame of hope, a promise that his dream wasn't lost, only delayed. And though it would take time, he knew that her voice, her presence, and her faith would be the pillars of his resilience.

Mahi's maturity and unwavering support stand out. She reassures Aarav with words full of understanding, offering him the freedom to focus on his dreams without the burden of constant communication. Her gentle reminder that she will be there for him, whether in presence or through virtual means, brings comfort to Aarav. In turn, Aarav finds a renewed sense of purpose, knowing he has a partner who understands the depth of his aspirations. This comfort fuels his commitment to his goals, yet he grapples with the inevitable pangs of jealousy as Mahi embraces new friendships and experiences. This duality captures a universal relationship struggle—the desire for closeness, coupled with the fear of growing apart as each partner pursues individual growth.

Their journey reflects the beauty of a relationship where two people are committed not just to each other but also to their own dreams. The chapter ends on a hopeful note, suggesting that while distance and challenges may arise, the foundation of their relationship—built on trust, resilience, and a shared vision for the future—will only strengthen over time.

Chapter 7: Breaking Boundaries

The emotional tension reaches a tipping point, causing a rift or a confrontation between them. In this pivotal chapter, they must confront their feelings and decide whether to adhere to the boundaries they initially set or allow their relationship to evolve beyond the contract.

As the sun dipped below the horizon, casting a golden hue over the city, the emotional tension between Aarav and Mahi reached a boiling point. For weeks, they had navigated their relationship with a careful balance of unspoken feelings and external expectations. Each interaction felt loaded, as if they were teetering on the edge of something monumental. And now, it was time to confront the reality they had both been avoiding.

It all began with a seemingly innocuous phone call. Aarav had been feeling increasingly anxious about Mahi's new life in Punjab. The more she flourished, the more he felt like a ghost in her life, a relic of her past. That evening, he dialled her number, hoping to connect and ground himself in their shared memories.

"Hey, Mahi! How's everything?" he asked, forcing a cheerful tone that didn't quite reach his heart.

"Hi, Aarav! Everything's going great. Just wrapped up a project with my study group," she replied, her voice bright but carrying an undercurrent of distraction.

"Good to hear! So, do you have any plans for the weekend?" He tried to keep the conversation light, but anxiety twisted in his stomach.

"Actually, we're planning to go out for dinner. A few friends and I want to explore the city," she said, excitement creeping into her tone.

Aarav's heart sank. "With your new friends? How about we video call instead? I'd love to catch up properly."

Mahi hesitated, sensing the shift in his tone. "Aarav, I really want to go. It's important for me to bond with them. I'll call you later, okay?"

The disappointment washed over him like a wave, but he masked it with a forced smile. "Sure. Just... don't forget about me, okay?"

"I won't," she assured him, but the words felt empty, both of them aware of the growing distance between them.

After they hung up, Aarav felt a storm of emotions brewing within him. He paced his small apartment, grappling with feelings of inadequacy and fear. Mahi was moving forward, carving a path for herself while he felt stuck in the shadows. The possessiveness that had once felt protective now gnawed at him, twisting into something darker.

Later that night, Mahi called him as promised, her voice cheerful. But as they talked, Aarav couldn't shake the unease that lingered. Mahi shared stories of her adventures, her excitement palpable, but he found himself feeling more like an outsider than ever.

"Sounds like you're having a blast," he remarked, trying to sound supportive. But his voice dripped with a hint of bitterness he couldn't contain.

"It's been amazing, Aarav! You should see the campus; it's so vibrant!" Mahi replied, but her enthusiasm only deepened his insecurities.

"I guess I'm just... worried. You're making all these new friends, and I can't help but feel like I'm being left behind." Aarav's vulnerability hung in the air, raw and exposed.

Mahi's expression shifted, and for a moment, he could hear the tension in her silence. "Aarav, this doesn't change what we have. I need you to trust me."

"Trust you?" Aarav shot back, frustration bubbling to the surface. "How can I trust you when you're out there living a life, I'm not part of? You're becoming someone I don't recognize."

Mahi's eyes narrowed, the hurt evident on her face. "And you're becoming someone I'm scared of, Aarav! This possessiveness—it's suffocating. I need space to grow."

The confrontation erupted like a volcano, the simmering tension bursting forth. They exchanged barbed words, each laced with years of pent-up emotions and unvoiced fears. Aarav felt his heart racing, a mix of anger and desperation spilling out.

"You wanted this, Mahi! You wanted to leave. I encouraged you to pursue your dreams, but now I feel like I'm losing you!" His voice trembled, the fear of abandonment surfacing with painful clarity.

"And I'm scared I'll lose myself if you keep trying to hold me back!" Mahi's words cut through him, sharp and accusatory. "I didn't sign up for this. I need to find my own way."

Silence fell between them, heavy and oppressive. The air crackled with unspoken emotions, and both felt the weight of the moment pressing down on them. Aarav's heart raced, a mixture of hurt and desperation spiralling within him.

"What do we do now?" he finally asked, his voice softer, the anger fading into vulnerability.

Mahi sighed, tears brimming in her eyes. "I don't know, Aarav. I care about you, but we're at a crossroads. We need to decide if we're going to stick to this... contract we created or if we're ready to let our relationship evolve."

The weight of her words hung between them, a stark reminder of the boundaries they had both agreed to. Aarav's heart ached

at the thought of losing her, yet he couldn't ignore the truth that lay before them. Their relationship had grown complex, intertwined with emotions they had both been too afraid to explore.

"I want to be there for you, but I can't keep living in fear of losing you," he confessed, his voice trembling. "I need to trust that you can make your own choices."

Mahi nodded, wiping away a tear. "And I need to trust that I can still have you in my life while I discover who I am. But we have to communicate. I can't handle the possessiveness. It's not healthy for either of us." In that moment, the boundaries they had established felt both constraining and necessary. They had built a foundation based on friendship and mutual support, but the emotional complexities of their relationship demanded revaluation.

"I'm scared, Mahi," Aarav admitted, his voice barely above a whisper. "I don't want to lose you. But I also don't want to hold you back."

Mahi leaned forward; her gaze intense. "Then let's redefine what we are. We don't have to adhere to some contract. We can be partners in this journey, supporting each other but allowing space for growth."

As they spoke, a sense of relief washed over Aarav. It was as if the dam holding back their emotions had finally broken. They could redefine their relationship, allowing it to evolve beyond the confines they had initially set.

"Okay," he said, his heart racing with hope. "Let's try. Let's be honest with each other about our feelings and fears."

Mahi smiled through her tears, a flicker of light breaking through the darkness that had enveloped them. "I want that, Aarav. I really do."

In that moment of vulnerability, they made a silent pact to confront their fears and embrace the journey ahead. No longer would they allow unspoken emotions to dictate their relationship. It was time to break free from the boundaries that had held them captive and forge a new path, together.

As they ended the call, both felt a sense of newfound clarity. The challenges ahead would not be easy, but they were ready to face them. Aarav realized that it was time to let go of his fears and embrace the possibility of change, while Mahi understood that independence did not mean sacrificing her connection with Aarav.

The emotional rift had catalysed a transformation, allowing them to emerge stronger and more united. They would navigate the complexities of their relationship with honesty and trust, ready to explore the unwritten chapters of their journey together.

Time seemed to blur as the months passed, and before Mahi knew it, her second semester had concluded with distinction in 2013. As part of the MBA curriculum, she was required to undertake a summer internship project, an opportunity that could shape her professional path. The college provided students with two choices: either they could secure their own internships, or the university would assign them one. Mahi, however, had made up her mind from the beginning. She wasn't going to wait for the college to place her somewhere random—no, she had Aarav, and she knew exactly who could help her find the perfect internship.

One evening, after wrapping up a late-night study session, Mahi called Aarav. She didn't hesitate. "Aarav, I need your help," she said, her voice soft but filled with determination. "I need to find a company for my summer internship. And I was thinking... maybe you could arrange something?"

Aarav's response was immediate, as if he had been waiting for this very moment. "Of course, Mahi," he replied, his voice warm, carrying the unmistakable hint of excitement. "I'll handle everything. You leave it to me."

Mahi's heart fluttered at the sound of his words. She knew what this meant. Aarav would make sure she didn't have to settle for anything less than the best. And more than that, she had a feeling—no, she was certain—that Aarav would ensure she'd be close to him. After a year of living apart, only seeing each other during short visits, the idea of spending two full months together was like a dream come true.

True to his promise, Aarav moved swiftly. Within days, Mahi received confirmation that she had secured an internship at Airlines in Lucknow, the very company where Aarav worked. But the beauty of it all was that Aarav had orchestrated things so perfectly—Mahi didn't even need to go into the office. She had her work assignments, her tasks, and her deadlines, but they could all be managed remotely. This meant more time together, more stolen moments where they could be just them—free from the constraints of time and obligations.

Every morning, Mahi would wake up with a smile on her face, knowing that her day wouldn't be filled with corporate meetings or mundane office work. Instead, she would spend her days with Aarav—laughing, talking, exploring the city, and deepening the bond they already shared. The summer unfolded like a magical interlude, a pause in the relentless pace of their lives where they could simply be with each other. The more time they spent together, the stronger their relationship grew, each day adding a new layer of understanding, trust, and love.

One evening, as the sun dipped below the horizon, painting the sky in hues of pink and orange, Mahi and Aarav sat on a rooftop terrace, watching the city come alive with lights. The warmth of Aarav's arm wrapped around her shoulders brought her a sense of peace she had never known before.

"Aarav," she said softly, her voice barely louder than a whisper, "Do you think we could go somewhere? Maybe take a trip together?"

Aarav turned to her, a curious smile on his face. "A trip?" he asked, his eyes twinkling with intrigue.

Mahi bit her lip, her eyes sparkling with the excitement of a long-held dream. "Yes... I've always wanted to visit Dehradun. It's been my dream to spend time in the mountains, away from everything, just you and me. What do you think?"

Aarav didn't need to think twice. The idea of spending time with Mahi, tucked away in the serene hills of Uttarakhand, sounded perfect. "Dehradun, huh?" he teased, brushing a strand of hair away from her face. "You know, I think that sounds like a perfect plan. We'll make it happen."

Mahi's heart swelled with happiness. Just the thought of walking through the misty hills, hand in hand with Aarav, felt like the perfect escape. They both had endured the long separation during her college semesters, but now, this trip felt like a chance to recharge—to reconnect with each other and with nature.

In the weeks leading up to the trip, Mahi's excitement grew. She would often find herself daydreaming about the two of them, nestled in a cozy cabin, watching the rain fall outside while the warmth of a crackling fire kept them close. She pictured the long drives through winding roads, the quiet moments of peace they'd share as they stood on hilltops, gazing out over the valleys below, their hearts filled with a shared love for the beauty around them.

When the day of the trip finally arrived, they packed their bags and set off, their excitement palpable in the air. As the car climbed higher into the hills, Mahi felt her heart lightening. The city, the noise, the distractions of everyday life—all of it seemed to fade away, leaving only the two of them, wrapped in the embrace of the mountains.

Dehradun greeted them with its misty mornings and lush greenery. Their days were spent exploring hidden trails, visiting serene monasteries, and indulging in quiet picnics by glistening rivers. The quiet serenity of the hills provided the perfect backdrop to their blossoming romance. Aarav was as attentive as ever, always finding ways to surprise Mahi—whether it was with a spontaneous candlelit dinner on the balcony of their hilltop lodge or a handwritten note slipped into her bag with simple, heartfelt words: I'm so glad we're here, together.

One evening, as they stood on a cliff, the cool breeze playing with Mahi's hair, Aarav wrapped his arms around her from behind. They stood in silence, watching as the sun dipped below the horizon, casting a golden glow over the landscape.

"I can't believe how perfect this is," Mahi whispered, leaning her head back against Aarav's chest. "I've always dreamed of moments like this, with you."

Aarav tightened his hold on her, pressing a soft kiss to her temple. "It's perfect because you're here," he said, his voice filled with sincerity. "I wouldn't want to be anywhere else."

As the sky faded from gold to deep indigo, dotted with stars, they stayed in that embrace—two souls who had found their way back to each other, time and again, through the twists and turns of life. In that serene private space, the mountains standing tall around them, they knew that whatever lay ahead, they would face it together.

For Mahi, this trip wasn't just a dream come true—it was a promise. A promise that no matter where life took them, no matter how unpredictable the journey, their love would remain their constant. It would be their unshakable foundation, a steady lighthouse in an ever-changing world.

One evening, as they wandered hand in hand along the winding mall Road in Mussoorie, the sky above painted in hues of pink and lavender, they shared not only laughs and smiles but dreams and hopes. Each step they took felt like a whispered promise, a quiet vow exchanged between two hearts that were growing more inseparable with every passing moment.

Mahi, her hair tousled by the gentle breeze, looked at Aarav with a quiet glow in her eyes. "Can we come back here again?" she asked softly, her voice barely above a whisper, as if she was afraid that speaking too loudly would break the spell this place had cast on them.

Aarav smiled, pulling her closer as they walked. "We'll come back, Mahi," he murmured, his gaze lingering on her face, the love in his eyes undeniable. "And not just once. Every time you want to escape the world, we'll find our way back here... together." When they returned from the trip to Lucknow, they carried with them memories that would last a lifetime—moments stolen in the quiet of the hills, conversations that wove their souls closer together, and promises whispered as they walked beneath the stars. They had shared not only their laughter but also their deepest fears, their vulnerabilities, and their hopes for what was to come. Their hearts, now entwined in ways they hadn't imagined, beat in sync as they left Dehradun behind. And as they moved forward into the uncertain future, they knew one thing for sure—together, they could face anything. Because in a world full of change, their love had become the one thing they could always rely on.

Part 4:
The Cross roads of Destiny

Chapter 8: A Serene Private Space

In the calm embrace of their secluded sanctuary, Aarav and Mahi find refuge from the outside world, discovering the power of shared silence.

Setting the Scene - A Private, Comfortable Space

It was July 21, 2013—Mahi's birthday. She had only one request for Aarav: to celebrate it together, just the two of them. And Aarav, always sensitive to her wishes, was determined to make the evening unforgettable. He planned the night meticulously, picking a restaurant known for its elegant atmosphere and exquisite food. It was the kind of place where memories were created under softly glowing chandeliers and where moments lingered in the air like sweet perfume.

As evening approached, Mahi arrived at the restaurant, dressed in a simple yet stunning Black outfit that made Aarav's heart flutter. She looked beautiful, radiant even, and he couldn't help but be awestruck by how effortlessly she carried herself. When he stood to greet her, her eyes lit up, and in that moment, he felt a swell of gratitude for simply being by her side.

The table he had reserved was adorned with soft candles casting a warm glow over everything, creating an ambiance that felt almost dreamlike. He had chosen every detail to make it perfect, from the music that played softly in the background to the quiet corner of the restaurant where they could enjoy each other's company without any interruptions. This was their moment, their evening.

A small cake sat at the center of the table, a simple but heartfelt gesture from Aarav. Mahi's eyes sparkled as she looked at it, and a gentle smile touched her lips. She blew out the candle, making a silent wish, and then cut the cake with Aarav by her side, her only company, exactly as she had wanted. As they shared the first slice, there was a quiet sense of intimacy between them, a feeling that this moment was just for them, a little pocket of time where nothing else mattered.

As they enjoyed the dessert, Mahi looked at Aarav with a twinkle in her eyes and confessed a small wish of hers that she had never voiced before. "I want to taste wine tonight. I've never had it, and today feels like the right time to try." She gave him a soft, playful smile.

Aarav chuckled, surprised but thrilled by her spontaneity. "It's your day, Mahi. Whatever you wish for, I'm here to make it happen." He ordered a glass of red wine for her and, for himself, some scotch, a drink he was more accustomed to.

As they sipped their drinks, the atmosphere between them softened even further. The wine warmed Mahi's cheeks, giving her a light blush that made her even more endearing to Aarav. They exchanged glances, each one speaking more than words ever could. The silence between them was comfortable, filled with the kind of warmth that only grows from truly knowing someone.

"Do you remember when we first met?" Mahi asked, her voice soft, a touch of nostalgia coloring her words. Aarav smiled, thinking back to that day when everything had started. "I do. You looked as beautiful then as you do now, maybe even more so tonight."

Mahi laughed, her laughter like a gentle melody that drifted over to Aarav. "You always know just what to say to make me smile," she murmured, her eyes meeting his with a warmth that made his heart beat just a bit faster.

They spent the next few moments sipping their drinks, trading memories and quiet smiles. The restaurant around them seemed to blur, fading into the background as they found themselves cocooned in their own little world. It was as though the rest of the world had melted away, leaving just the two of them suspended in a space of their own.

Then, as if reading his thoughts, Mahi turned to him with a suggestion that caught him off guard. "Let's take a walk," she whispered, her eyes gleaming with excitement. "Let's get some fresh air, just you and me."

Aarav didn't hesitate. He took her hand, and together they left the restaurant, stepping into the quiet night. The streets were bathed in a soft, golden light, and the night air was cool against their skin. They walked side by side, their fingers brushing occasionally, sending a spark through both of them each time.

Without realizing where they were going, they found themselves by a small, quiet park. It was almost deserted, with only the sound of rustling leaves and a faint breeze to accompany them. Aarav led her to a bench, and they sat, gazing up at the stars that dotted the night sky.

"Thank you for tonight," Mahi whispered, her voice barely more than a breath. "This is exactly what I wanted. Just you and me. Nothing more, nothing less."

Aarav turned to look at her, feeling a wave of emotion swell within him. "There's nothing I wouldn't do to make you happy, Mahi. Being here with you, sharing this moment... it's everything to me."

In the silence that followed, Mahi reached out, intertwining her fingers with his. The gesture was simple, but it spoke volumes. It was as if, in that moment, all her feelings, all the unspoken words, were communicated through that single touch.

They sat like that for a long time, content just to be in each other's presence. Occasionally, they would exchange a glance, a small smile, or a soft squeeze of the hand, each gesture deepening the connection between them. The world around them faded into insignificance, and time seemed to slow, leaving just the two of them in a bubble of peace and contentment.

After a while, Mahi turned to him with a shy smile. "Aarav, do you think... do you think we'll always be like this? Just the two of us, finding these little moments?"

Aarav looked into her eyes, his own gaze steady and filled with warmth. "As long as you're by my side, Mahi, I don't need anything else. I don't know what the future holds, but I know I want you to be a part of it."

The words hung between them, heavy with meaning. For a moment, Mahi looked as though she might cry, her eyes glistening with unshed tears. But then she smiled, a smile so radiant that it took Aarav's breath away.

They continued talking, sharing dreams, fears, and hopes, all in the quiet intimacy of that starlit night. By the time they decided to head back, the air between them was filled with a newfound sense of closeness. It was as though they had peeled back yet another layer of their souls, revealing parts of themselves that had been hidden even from each other.

As they walked back, Aarav felt a surge of affection for the woman by his side. He wanted to hold onto this moment forever, to keep it close and cherish it, knowing that it was a memory he would carry with him for the rest of his life.

And Sudden Mahi Said, Aarav....

"I want to stay at your place tonight," she said softly, her voice filled with both certainty and a touch of vulnerability. Her internship in Lucknow was drawing to a close, and they both knew that soon, their days spent together in the same city would come to an end. Mahi wanted to hold on to every moment they had left.

Aarav looked at her, surprised but not in disbelief. It had been two years since they had first confessed their love for each other, and in that time, they had created a world of their own. Late-night conversations, moments of laughter, quiet evenings spent just being with each other—all of it had brought them closer in ways words couldn't describe. But tonight felt different. There was an intimacy between them, something unspoken, that filled the air. Without hesitation, Aarav nodded, his eyes softening as he smiled. "Let's go," he said, his voice quiet but filled with a sense of anticipation.

They reached at Aarav's apartment, a familiar place for both of them. The soft glow of the lamps bathed the room in a warm, golden light, and the sound of soft music filled the background, creating a serene atmosphere. They had just finished a quiet dinner, but neither of them seemed eager to move from the couch where they sat close together.

Mahi leaned into Aarav, her head resting on his shoulder as his arm wrapped around her, pulling her in a little tighter. She could feel the steady rise and fall of his chest and the warmth of his skin where their bodies touched. There was a comfort in the silence they shared, but beneath it, there was something else—a sense of anticipation, of unspoken desire that had been building for some time.

Aarav shifted slightly, turning his head to press a gentle kiss to the top of Mahi's head. "You're quiet tonight," he murmured, his voice soft and low.

Mahi smiled against his shoulder, her fingers tracing absent patterns on his arm. "Just thinking," she replied, her voice barely above a whisper. She tilted her head up to meet his gaze, her eyes searching his face for a moment before she spoke again. "I think...I'm ready."

The weight of her words hung in the air between them, heavy with meaning. Aarav's eyes darkened slightly as he understood what she meant. He had always respected her pace, never rushing her, but the desire had always been there, simmering just beneath the surface.

"Are you sure?" he asked softly, his hand moving to gently cup her cheek, his thumb brushing lightly over her skin.

Mahi nodded, her heart racing, but there was no hesitation in her eyes. "Yes," she whispered. "I want this, Aarav. I want you."

The Slow Build - Tenderness and Anticipation

Aarav's heart swelled at her words, his love for her almost overwhelming in that moment. He leaned in slowly, capturing her lips in a soft, lingering kiss. There was no rush, no urgency—just a slow, deliberate exploration, as if they were savoring the taste of each other for the first time.

Mahi responded with the same tenderness, her lips moving against his in perfect sync. She could feel the warmth of his body pressing against hers, the steady beat of his heart beneath her palm. As the kiss deepened, she allowed herself to melt into him, her arms wrapping around his neck as she pulled him closer.

Aarav's hands moved to her waist; his touch gentle yet firm as he guided her onto his lap. She straddled him, their bodies now fully pressed together, and she could feel the heat of his desire between them. But still, there was no rush. This moment was about more than just physical need—it was about trust, about opening themselves up to each other in a way they hadn't before. He broke the kiss to trail soft kisses along her jawline, his breath warm against her skin. Mahi tilted her head back, her eyes fluttering shut as his lips traveled down to the sensitive spot on her neck. Her breath hitched slightly, and she could feel a shiver of anticipation run down her spine.

"Aarav..." she whispered, her fingers threading through his hair, pulling him closer as if she couldn't get enough of him.

"I've got you," he murmured against her skin, his voice low and husky. His hands moved under her shirt, the feel of his fingertips on her bare skin sending sparks of electricity through her. Slowly, deliberately, he peeled the shirt over her head, discarding it on the floor before his hands returned to explore the newly exposed skin.

Exploration - Sensual and Deliberate

Mahi's heart pounded in her chest as Aarav's hands roamed her body with a slow, purposeful touch. His fingertips traced the curve of her spine, the dip of her waist, the softness of her stomach, learning her as if she were a map he was memorizing by heart. He looked at her like she was the most beautiful thing he had ever seen, his eyes filled with awe and tenderness.

"You're perfect," he whispered, his voice reverent as he leaned in to kiss her again, his lips brushing against hers with a tenderness that made her heart ache.

Mahi could feel the heat rising between them, the slow burn of desire turning into something deeper, more intense. She wanted him—every part of him. She wanted to feel him, to be closer to him than she had ever been before.

Her hands moved to the hem of his shirt, and with a slight tug, Aarav helped her pull it over his head, discarding it beside hers. She ran her hands over his chest, feeling the taut muscles beneath his skin, the way his breath hitched slightly at her touch. The sensation of his bare skin against hers was intoxicating, and she couldn't help but press herself closer to him, craving the warmth of his body.

Aarav's hands moved to the clasp of her hairs, his movements slow, deliberate, giving her plenty of time to stop him if she wanted to. But she didn't. She nodded slightly, giving him silent permission to continue, and with a soft click, the fabric fell away, leaving her exposed to him for the first time.

He pulled back slightly to look at her, his eyes dark and filled with desire, but also with something else—something deeper, more profound. Love. Respect. Devotion.

"You're beautiful," he whispered, his hands moving to cup her neck, his thumbs brushing lightly over her sensitive skin. Mahi gasped at the sensation, her body arching into his touch.

Intimacy - Connection and Fulfilment

Their movements grew slower, more deliberate, as they explored each other with a tenderness that spoke of their deep emotional connection. There was no rush, no frantic need—just the slow, steady build of desire that had been growing between them for years.

Aarav's hands travelled lower, his touch sending shivers down Mahi's spine as he explored every inch of her body, learning what made her gasp, what made her breath hitch, what made her melt into him. And Mahi responded in kind, her hands tracing the lines of his body, her touch soft and reverent as she explored him with the same curiosity and desire.

When the moment finally came, when they were fully connected in a way they hadn't been before, it was like everything else fell away. There was no room for hesitation, no space for doubt—only the overwhelming sensation of being completely and utterly consumed by each other.

Their movements were slow, deliberate, as they reveled in the intimacy of the moment, their bodies moving together in perfect harmony. It was more than just physical—it was emotional, spiritual, as if they were two halves of the same whole, finally coming together after years of longing.

Mahi's breath came in soft gasps, her body trembling beneath Aarav's as they reached the peak of their shared desire. And when they finally found release, it wasn't just a physical culmination—it was the fulfilment of everything they had been building together for the past two years.

As they lay there afterward, tangled together in each other's arms, their bodies still humming with the afterglow of their intimacy, there was a sense of peace that settled over them. It wasn't just the act itself that had been significant—it was the trust, the vulnerability, the love that had made the moment so perfect.

Aarav kissed the top of Mahi's head, his arms

tightening around her as if to reassure her that he wasn't going anywhere.

"I love you," he whispered, his voice soft and filled with emotion.

Mahi smiled against his chest; her eyes fluttering shut as she pressed a kiss to his skin. *"I love you too."* And in that moment, as they held each other close, they knew that this was only the beginning of something even more beautiful.

But as dawn broke and the first rays of sunlight filtered through the curtains, reality had come too quickly. The night they had shared was over, and they both knew it. As they stood now at the train station, ready to part once again, the weight of the distance between them settled heavily on their hearts. Mahi was headed back to her hostel, and Aarav had to return to Lucknow. Yet, even though they were about to be apart, a part of him remained with her—just as a part of her would stay with him.

He still felt the warmth of her body, her scent mingling with his, lingering on his clothes and skin. Over the next few days, they would talk often, their conversations filled with the memory of their time together. They would replay those moments over and over, savoring every detail, every feeling, as if trying to hold on to the night they had shared.

And despite the challenges, the miles that stretched between them, their love remained—complex, evolving, but always present. For Mahi and Aarav, the night had been a chapter, but it wasn't the end of their story. It was a promise of more to come, a testament to the strength of what they had built.

As the train pulled away from the station, Mahi waved, her heart full but aching at the same time. Aarav stood there, watching her disappear from sight, but even as the train left, he knew that this was far from the end. Their journey was just beginning.

Chapter 9: A New Understanding

In the final chapter, the boy and girl come to a resolution. They reassess their relationship, deciding whether to break free from the contractual nature of their bond and embrace a deeper connection, or part ways. This chapter wraps up their journey, focusing on their personal growth and mutual understanding.

The early morning light filtered through Mahi's dorm window, illuminating the space with a soft glow. She sat at her desk, surrounded by books and notes, yet her mind was elsewhere, replaying the conversation with Aarav from the night before. It was a pivotal moment, a reckoning that had shifted the very foundation of their relationship.

Aarav, too, was lost in thought. Back in Lucknow, he stared out of his apartment window, the bustling streets below mirroring the chaos within him. The weight of their emotional confrontation lingered, but for the first time, he felt a flicker of hope. Their relationship didn't have to be defined by fear and possessiveness; it could grow into something deeper, more meaningful.

As the days passed, Mahi threw herself into her studies, but her heart remained tethered to the unresolved feelings for Aarav. Their late-night calls became more frequent, filled with laughter and stories, yet each conversation hinted at the deeper connection they were both yearning for. The boundaries they had previously established felt increasingly irrelevant, as if they were mere walls restricting their potential.

One evening, during a video call, Mahi looked into Aarav's eyes, searching for clarity. "I've been thinking a lot about us," she began, her heart racing. "About what it means to be together but also to be individuals."

Aarav nodded, his expression earnest. "I've thought about it too. It's clear we care about each other deeply, but I realize I need to let you have your space. You're growing, and I want to support that."

Mahi felt a wave of relief wash over her. "And I need you to know that my growth doesn't mean I care about you any less. I want to redefine what we have, to embrace this connection without fear."

Their words hung in the air, a gentle acknowledgment of the shift in their relationship. Aarav's heart swelled at the thought of supporting Mahi in her journey, and he felt the burden of possessiveness lift. "So, what does that look like for us?" he asked, genuinely curious.

"I think we can still be a part of each other's lives while allowing for independence," Mahi replied thoughtfully. "We don't have to put labels on everything. Maybe we can just enjoy the journey together."

Aarav smiled, the tension in his chest easing. "I like that. It feels right."

With this newfound understanding, they began to explore the depths of their relationship. They shared more about them aspirations, their fears, and the dreams they had yet to chase. Mahi spoke passionately about her coursework, the new friends she was making, and her aspirations for a future in aviation. Aarav, in turn, discussed his ambitions within the airline industry, hoping to climb the ranks and create a lasting impact.

Yet, even as they grew closer, old habits were hard to shake. Aarav sometimes found himself slipping back into worry whenever Mahi mentioned spending time with her new friends. "Are you sure you won't forget about me?" he would ask, half-joking, half-serious.

Mahi would laugh, but there was a depth to her smile. "How could I? You're a part of this journey, Aarav. Just because I'm meeting new people doesn't mean I'm leaving you behind."

Over time, the conversations shifted from apprehension to excitement. They began to dream together, envisioning a future

that included both their paths. They shared silly aspirations—Mahi wanting to be a pilot flying international routes, and Aarav hoping to open his own travel agency one day.

One weekend, Mahi invited Aarav to visit her in Punjab. It was a significant step, symbolizing a merging of their worlds. When he arrived, the campus buzzed with life, and Mahi introduced him to her friends. Aarav felt a mixture of pride and anxiety, but Mahi's warm smile reassured him.

"Just be yourself," she whispered as they walked into the bustling cafeteria. "They're going to love you."

Throughout the day, Aarav observed Mahi in her element, navigating her new environment with ease. She laughed freely, her confidence shining through. Watching her thrive filled him with joy, but it also highlighted the journey he had taken alongside her.

As the day turned into night, they found themselves sitting on the campus lawn, the stars twinkling overhead. The atmosphere was electric, filled with laughter from nearby groups of students, but it was just the two of them in their own world.

"Mahi," Aarav began, the seriousness of his tone pulling her focus. "I'm really proud of you. You've grown so much since we first met."

Mahi's cheeks flushed with warmth. "Thank you, Aarav. I couldn't have done this without your support. You believed in me when I didn't believe in myself."

He shifted closer, feeling a connection that was palpable. "And I need you to know that your growth inspires me. I want to be a better person for you, for myself."

Mahi smiled, her heart swelling. "Then let's continue to support each other, no matter where life takes us. We can be there for one another while still embracing our independence."

Aarav nodded, their hands brushing against each other, sending sparks through the air. "Together, then. No more boundaries, just understanding."

In that moment, they both knew they had reached a pivotal point in their relationship. It was no longer about the contractual bond they had initially established; it was about genuine connection, trust, and mutual respect. They were ready to embark on this journey together, free from the constraints of fear.

As the weeks turned into months, Aarav and Mahi continued to nurture their relationship. They communicated openly, celebrating each other's successes and navigating challenges together. Mahi completed her first semester with top marks, and

Aarav was promoted at work, both of them buoyed by the other's encouragement.

Their connection blossomed, evolving from a simple friendship into something more profound. The playful banter remained, but it was laced with deeper affection. Aarav would send Mahi small gifts and handwritten notes, while Mahi surprised him with homemade meals whenever he visited. They learned to balance their ambitions with their feelings, crafting a relationship that was uniquely their own.

During Diwali vacation, Mahi returned to Lucknow, eager to embrace the festive warmth of home. The city gleamed with the glow of diyas, casting a golden hue on every corner, while the air danced with the scent of sweets and the cheer of celebration. Aarav, about to leave for his hometown, made a special stop at Mahi's house before his journey. He carried a basket of gifts and sweets, not only for her but for her family—a gesture of care and affection that had grown deeper with time.

Mahi welcomed him with a smile that lit up brighter than the diyas surrounding them. They exchanged stories of the past few weeks, laughter mingling with the sounds of distant firecrackers. Aarav's gift was simple, yet it carried with it a weight of affection and unspoken care. Aarav's gift was simple—a reflection of his quiet but deep affection for Mahi, and as she accepted it, her heart swelled with warmth.

Over the Diwali holidays, Aarav introduced Mahi to his family, sharing her photographs with his mother. His mother, instantly drawn to Mahi's charm, couldn't contain her excitement and asked, "I'd love to talk to her!" Aarav, gently smiling, told his mother that Mahi might be busy with the festival but assured her they would meet soon.

After Diwali, as Aarav returned to Lucknow, life resumed its normal rhythm, yet something had subtly shifted between them. One evening, they sat on the balcony of Mahi's dorm, overlooking the cityscape sparkling with lights. The cool breeze brushed past them, but neither felt the chill. Aarav, his gaze soft and filled with something unspoken, turned toward Mahi.

"You know," he began, his voice calm and steady, "I never imagined I'd find someone who inspires me as much as you do."

Mahi looked at him, her eyes reflecting the gentle glow of the distant streetlights. "And I never thought I could be this happy while chasing my dreams. It's like we're growing together, not apart," she replied softly, her voice laced with a warmth that mirrored her feelings.

Aarav asked to Mahi and wanted to say something...

Mahi said, yes...

Aarav took a breath, his heart racing slightly. "I told my mother about you."

Mahi's eyes widened, a flicker of surprise crossing her face. "What? What did you tell her?" she asked, her voice tinged with nervous curiosity.

Aarav smiled, sensing her unease. "Just about our relationship."

Mahi's heart quickened as she leaned forward. "And? What was her reaction?"

"She's just like me," Aarav said with a casual shrug, his smile widening. "She liked you. I showed her some photos of us together, told her a bit about you. She even wanted to talk to you, but I told her you were busy with the festival. I promised her we'd meet soon."

Mahi's breath steadied, and she let out a small sigh of relief, her lips curving into a gentle smile.

Their hands, almost instinctively, found each other, fingers intertwining in a way that felt both new and familiar. It was a silent promise—a vow to face the future together, despite the uncertainties. In that moment, they weren't just holding hands; they were holding onto hope, dreams, and the unspoken understanding that love wasn't about possession, but about giving each other wings to soar.

As they sat beneath the expanse of the starlit sky, their conversation softened into quiet murmurs. It wasn't just words they shared, but fragments of their dreams, their hopes, and their laughter—drifting softly into the night. The stars twinkled above them, much like the countless possibilities that lay ahead, illuminating the boundless road of their future.

In that tender silence, they came to a shared understanding: their love wasn't about holding each other back, but about lifting one another higher. It was a love built on mutual respect, a space where they could both grow—individually, yet always intertwined. It wasn't about possession, but about the freedom to chase their ambitions while staying connected at the heart.

As they sat close, basking in the stillness of the night, fear and doubt seemed to fade into nothingness. Only the vastness of their future remained, stretching out before them—just as endless as the sky above. Their journey had only just begun, with so much yet to unfold.

But reality had a way of intruding upon even the most perfect moments. As their vacation drew to a close, the same night Mahi had to leave for her university. They lingered a little longer under the stars, savoring the final few hours before they had to part once again. Though miles would separate them, both knew that the love they nurtured on nights like these would be the anchor, guiding them forward.

The next morning, the soft golden light of the sun filtered through Mahi's dorm window. She sat at her desk, her books and notes spread out before her, but her mind lingered on the night before. She replayed Aarav's words, the warmth in his voice, and the way they had sat together, their hands clasped. It wasn't just a memory; it was a promise. A promise to walk this path hand in hand, no matter where life would take them next

Aarav, too, was lost in thought. Back in Lucknow, he stared out of his apartment window, the bustling streets below mirroring the chaos within him. The weight of their emotional confrontation lingered, but for the first time, he felt a flicker of hope. Their relationship didn't have to be defined by fear and possessiveness; it could grow into something deeper, more meaningful.

As the days passed, Mahi threw herself into her studies, but her heart remained tethered to the unresolved feelings for Aarav. Their late-night calls became more frequent, filled with laughter and stories, yet each conversation hinted at the deeper connection they were both yearning for. The boundaries they had previously established felt increasingly irrelevant, as if they were mere walls restricting their potential.

One evening, during a video call, Mahi looked into Aarav's eyes, searching for clarity. "I've been thinking a lot about us," she began, her heart racing. "About what it means to be together but also to be individuals."

As Aarav was engrossed in his UPSC preparation and managing the demands of his airline job, he found himself gradually drifting away from Mahi. His packed schedule left him little time for deep conversations, and although Mahi would often call him, the conversations were brief, almost mechanical. Aarav would talk for a while, distracted, then hang up, leaving Mahi feeling more and more distant. Frustrated and hurt, she finally poured her feelings into an email, hoping it would convey the weight of her emotions better than her fleeting phone calls.

In the email, Mahi's heart was laid bare:

"I'm upset, truly. Ever since you came home this morning, you haven't really talked to me. Not once have we had a proper conversation. Please, Aarav, I need you to understand. Brushing things off as a joke is fine sometimes, but lately...

I've been thinking a lot about us—about you, about me, about everything."

Her words expressed a deeper frustration, a longing for connection that was slipping away. Mahi admitted to feeling confused, unsure of how she could navigate a future with Aarav if he continued to emotionally distance himself. The thought of building a life together without genuine communication weighed heavily on her, creating an anxiety that she couldn't ignore.

"I'm confused, Aarav. I don't know how I'll manage to spend my whole life with you if you continue like this. If you won't seriously listen to me, how can I ever be sure about our future together? It's starting to make me anxious. I'm struggling to figure out what I want in life, and on top of that, there's you. You never truly listen, never open up about anything serious on your own."

Mahi wasn't just upset about the immediate lack of communication, but about a deeper disconnect that had grown between them. She needed reassurance, but she also needed Aarav to understand her perspective.

"Aarav, I really want us to talk—about you, about me, about the life we're building. Please, think about this. I'm writing this email because you don't listen when I call, and I can't keep bottling it up. Please, read this fully and call me, whether now or later. But most importantly, think about it, Aarav."

Her vulnerability shone through in her final lines. Mahi wasn't accusing him of anything malicious; she was simply reaching out, hoping that he would finally hear her—truly hear her—and respond in a way that showed he cared.

"I'm really stressed out, not just with home and everything else that's happening, but with my own thoughts. My mind is a mess right now. Aarav, I love you. Please don't misunderstand me, but I'm really confused about how we'll make it work for the rest of our lives. I need you to understand, please. I love you so much."

The email was a plea—a quiet, emotional request for the connection they once had, for a future that wasn't just built on love but on understanding and communication. Mahi had put her heart into the message, hoping Aarav would take it seriously, hoping it would be the beginning of a deeper conversation they both desperately needed.

Aarav replied her back through email... *I know things feel uncertain right now, but there's absolutely no need to worry. You are, and always will be, the most important person in my life. My heart is with you every moment, and that will never change. I've been thinking a lot about us, and even though I missed the UPSC Mains last time, I can't afford to lose this opportunity again. But I want you to know, my love for you is never something I'll let go of, no matter what happens. I'm right here—always with you.*

I've also realized something important. We care about each other more than words can express, but I understand you're on your own path. You're growing into the person you were always meant to be, and I admire that. I admire you. I don't want to hold you back in any way, so I'll give you the space you need to chase your dreams, just like you've always supported mine.

But know this, no distance, no time apart, will ever change how I feel about you. You are my heart, and I'll always be by your side, cheering you on, whether I'm standing right next to you or watching from a far.

Mahi felt a wave of relief wash over her. "And I need you to know that my growth doesn't mean I care about you any less. I want to redefine what we have, to embrace this connection without fear."

Their words hung in the air, a gentle acknowledgment of the shift in their relationship. Aarav's heart swelled at the thought of supporting Mahi in her journey, and he felt the burden of possessiveness lift. "So, what does that look like for us?" he asked, genuinely curious.

"I think we can still be a part of each other's lives while allowing for independence," Mahi replied thoughtfully. "We don't have to put labels on everything. Maybe we can just enjoy the journey together."

Aarav smiled, the tension in his chest easing. "I like that. It feels right."

With this newfound understanding, they began to explore the depths of their relationship. They shared more about their aspirations, their fears, and the dreams they had yet to chase. Mahi spoke passionately about her coursework, the new friends she was making, and her aspirations for a future in aviation. Aarav, in turn, discussed his ambitions within the airline industry, hoping to climb the ranks and create a lasting impact.

Yet, even as they grew closer, old habits were hard to shake. Aarav sometimes found himself slipping back into worry whenever Mahi mentioned spending time with her new friends. "Are you sure you won't forget about me?" he would ask, half-joking, half-serious.

Mahi would laugh, but there was a depth to her smile. "How could I? You're a part of this journey, Aarav. Just because I'm meeting new people doesn't mean I'm leaving you behind."

Over time, the conversations shifted from apprehension to excitement. They began to dream together, envisioning a future that included both their paths. They shared silly aspirations—Mahi wanting to be a pilot flying international routes, and Aarav hoping to open his own travel agency one day.

In that moment, they both realized that love didn't have to be defined by possessiveness or constraints; it could flourish in the freedom of mutual understanding and support. Their journey together had only just begun, and the possibilities ahead were as limitless as the sky above.

Chapter 10: Silent Departures

" The chapter opens with a reflective tone, capturing the essence of Aarav and Mahi's relationship as it stands on the brink of change. It begins in the vibrant city of Delhi, bustling with opportunities yet tinged with the bittersweet reality of their impending separation. Aarav, now accustomed to the fast pace of city life, recalls the moments spent with Mahi during her training at the textile retail MNC."

The Initial Connection

After Mahi completed her MBA in 2014, she landed a job with a well-known textile retailer in Delhi from Campus placement. As Mahi settled into her new job, life seemed to follow a rhythm that was comforting yet tinged with longing. Her days in Delhi had been a whirlwind of training, meetings, and navigating the corporate world. The city, vast and vibrant, offered her the promise of a grand future. The busy streets of Connaught Place and the allure of India Gate at night filled her with a sense of belonging. But amidst the hustle of her rising career, Aarav had become her anchor.

Every weekend, Aarav would catch the earliest flight or train from Lucknow to Delhi. Their time together was a mix of excitement and familiarity. They would wander through the narrow lanes of Old Delhi, savoring the aroma of street food, lost in the charm of centuries-old architecture. Then, at sunset, they'd find themselves at the latest café or restaurant, surrounded by the city's modern pulse. Each meeting was magical, filled with laughter, long conversations, and unspoken emotions. Aarav reveled in these moments, holding on to the fleeting time they spent together, while Mahi's mind wandered between the present and her future aspirations.

But as weeks turned into months, the distance began to weigh heavily on Aarav. The journeys were not just physically exhausting but emotionally draining. Each goodbye seemed harder than the last. One evening, as they sat in a quiet corner of their favorite café in Laxmi Nagar, Delhi, sipping coffee under the dim lights, Aarav gently took Mahi's hand.

"Mahi, I love these weekends with you," he began, his voice soft yet firm. "But every time I leave, it feels like I'm losing a piece of myself. I want to be closer to you, not just in moments but every day. Could you think about transferring to Lucknow? Or maybe somewhere nearby?"

Mahi looked at him, her heart heavy. She knew how much Aarav cherished their time together, and truthfully, she did too. The thought of being closer to him, of not having to part ways every Sunday evening, was tempting. But deep down, she also knew that her ambition, her dreams, were calling her in a different direction. Yet for now, she chose to ease Aarav's burden.

"Let me see what I can do," she replied, her smile gentle but unsure.

A few weeks later, the news came. Mahi had managed to secure a transfer to Allahabad, a city much closer to Lucknow. It wasn't perfect, but it was a compromise. Aarav was overjoyed. No longer would he have to endure the long trips to Delhi. Allahabad was just a few hours away, making their weekend reunions far more frequent and less rushed.

Their first weekend in Allahabad was filled with a new kind of excitement. They explored the ancient city, visited its temples, and sat by the river, watching the boats drift lazily under the sun. The time they spent together now felt more relaxed, and their conversations flowed more freely, unburdened by the ticking clock of a long-distance relationship. Aarav's heart was full, content in the thought that they were now closer than ever before.

But as the weeks passed, Aarav began to sense a restlessness in Mahi. She was happy to be closer to him, but there was something deeper, something unsaid that lingered in her eyes. One evening, as they sat by the river, Aarav asked her, "Mahi, are you truly happy here? I feel like something's bothering you."

Mahi looked away, gazing at the horizon, her fingers gently tracing the edge of her coffee cup. "I am, Aarav. I love being with you, and these weekends are precious to me. But…"

Aarav's heart sank as she hesitated, the weight of her words hanging in the air.

"But I can't ignore this feeling inside me. I love what I do, but I also want more. I want to reach higher, to explore more opportunities. And sometimes, I feel like I'm compromising too much, not for myself but for us."

Aarav's grip on her hand tightened, not in frustration but in understanding. He knew that Mahi had always been ambitious, driven by dreams larger than the confines of any one city. Her time in Delhi had opened doors for her, doors that perhaps Allahabad or even Lucknow couldn't. He had hoped that being closer would make things easier, but it had only made her desire for growth more evident.

"Mahi, I don't want to hold you back," Aarav whispered, his voice breaking ever so slightly. "If you feel like you need to go, to chase something bigger, I won't stop you."

Tears welled up in Mahi's eyes, not from sadness but from the depth of Aarav's love. She leaned her head against his shoulder, breathing in the warmth of the moment. "I don't know what's ahead, Aarav. But right now, I just want to be with you, no matter what happens."

And in that moment, under the fading light of the sun, they both understood that while love could fill their hearts, ambition and dreams could never be silenced.

During one of their conversations, she revealed her ambitions: "Aarav, I don't want to limit myself to India. I want to fly, to explore the world." Her eyes sparkled with a mix of excitement and fear.

This revelation stirred something within Aarav. He admired Mahi's determination but was also aware of the implications. They began discussing her plans more seriously. "You need a passport and visa," he mentioned, trying to support her dreams. To his surprise, she turned to him, her voice steady. "Can you help me with that?"

With Aarav unwavering support, Mahi secured her passport and visa, and soon enough, she boarded a flight to Dubai for job hunting. Mahi arrived in Dubai, full of anticipation but quickly faced the harsh reality of the job market. Days turned into weeks without any positive response. Aarav worried about her, often calling to check in. Each time, Mahi reassured him, "I'm okay, Aarav. Just a matter of time." Yet, he could hear the fatigue in her voice. You can do this!" His encouragement meant the world to her. Aarav was proud of her courage but couldn't shake the feeling of impending loss. They promised to stay connected, but each time they spoke, he sensed a growing distance.

Ten days passed, and the distance between them grew palpable. One day, Aarav received a call from Mahi. "Aarav, I'm struggling to get interviews here. Can you help?" Her voice was tinged with frustration, and Aarav felt a pang of sympathy. He knew her well enough to understand the pressure she was under. Mahi had an idea. Knowing Aarav's cousin lived in Dubai, she suggested, "Can your cousin help me network?" Aarav wasted no time reaching out to his cousin, who was eager to assist. "I'll set up a meeting for you, Mahi," he promised, feeling a surge of hope for her but just when Mahi began to lose faith, she received a call for an interview at a prestigious bank from Dubai. The news brought excitement, and she shared it with Aarav, who celebrated her achievement. "This is your chance, Mahi!

Mahi prepared rigorously, pouring over research and practicing her answers with the help of Aarav. On the day of the interview, she felt a mix of anxiety and determination. "This could change everything," she told Aarav as they spoke the night before. The interview went well, and she left feeling hopeful. After what felt like an eternity, Mahi returned to India, still processing the whirlwind of her Dubai experience. They met in Lucknow, where Mahi recounted her stories of the bustling city, the vibrant culture, and her interview at the bank. Aarav listened intently, proud of her accomplishments yet aware of the subtle distance that had begun to creep in.

Aarav and Mahi had spent countless weekends together, cherishing each moment as they reminisced about old memories and made plans for the future. It had been their ritual—a sanctuary amidst the chaos of their lives. But as time passed, Aarav couldn't help but reflect on his own stalled ambitions. Two years earlier, he had taken a shot at the UPSC exams, only to face setbacks that left him feeling stuck.

"I'll focus on my studies once you settle," Aarav had promised Mahi one evening, a quiet determination in his voice. She had nodded in agreement, understanding the depth of his sacrifice. Aarav had even switched his job from the airline industry to academics, hoping the change would give him the time and space to fully concentrate on his UPSC dream.

Then, one morning, everything changed.

Mahi's phone chimed with an email notification as she sat in her office. It was from the prestigious bank in Dubai where she had applied months ago. Her hands trembled as she opened it, her heart racing. The words blurred on the screen, but one sentence stood out clearly: Offer of Employment. Mahi's breath caught in her throat. Her dream job. She had finally made it.

Without a second thought, she dialled Aarav's number, her heart pounding with excitement and a hint of dread. But when the call went unanswered, she remembered he was in the middle of a lecture. Disappointed but understanding, she left him a message and waited.

Later that afternoon, Aarav finally finished his class and saw her missed call. He quickly dialled her back, eager to hear her voice. When Mahi answered, she didn't waste a second.

"Aarav, I got the job! My dream job!" Her voice bubbled with elation, the excitement practically leaping through the phone.

Aarav's heart swelled with pride, but beneath the joy, something darker stirred. Her words hit him like a wave, and for a brief moment, he struggled to find his voice.

"That's incredible, Mahi," he managed to say, forcing a smile even though she couldn't see it. "I'm so happy for you."

And he was. He was proud of her, deeply proud of everything she had achieved. But beneath that pride lay a gnawing sorrow. The job in Dubai meant one thing—distance. Another long stretch of separation, just as they had endured during her MBA days. Only this time, it felt more permanent. More real.

Mahi's voice softened as if she sensed the heaviness in his words. "Are you okay, Aarav?" she asked gently. "I want you to be happy, truly."

"I am happy," he replied, though his voice faltered slightly. "It's just... I wish we weren't going to be so far apart again."

Silence hung between them for a moment, both grappling with the reality of their situation. They had survived distance before, but this felt different, more daunting.

Later that day, Mahi decided she needed to see him. Without hesitation, she packed a bag and boarded a bus to Lucknow. She wanted to be there with Aarav, to share her news in person, to celebrate not just through a phone call but by being by his side. The journey felt longer than usual, her mind filled with excitement and uncertainty.

When she arrived, Aarav greeted her with a warm hug, holding her tightly as if afraid she might slip away. That evening, they celebrated her success with their friends, the laughter and joy of the moment masking the tension that lingered between them. But once the party ended, and they found themselves alone under the stars, the conversation they had been avoiding finally surfaced.

Aarav turned to Mahi; his gaze soft but burdened with unspoken fears. "You're settled now, Mahi," he began quietly. "And I'm so proud of you. But... now I need to focus on my own dream. My UPSC attempt. I've put it off for too long."

Mahi reached out and took his hand in hers, their fingers intertwining as she looked into his eyes. "I understand, Aarav. You've been there for me through everything. Now, it's your turn. I'll support you, no matter what."

But Aarav's heart was heavy. "I'm scared, Mahi," he admitted, his voice barely above a whisper. "What if this time, the distance is too much? What if... we can't make it work?"

Mahi squeezed his hand, her eyes filled with determination. "We've faced distance before, Aarav. We'll face it again. We're stronger than that."

Her words were meant to reassure him, but the fear still gnawed at the edges of his heart. He pulled her close, resting his forehead against hers as the quiet night wrapped around them.

"I love you, Mahi," he whispered, his voice thick with emotion. "More than anything."

"And I love you," she whispered back, her breath warm against his skin.

They stood there, wrapped in each other's arms, the future uncertain but their love unwavering. It was a bittersweet moment, filled with both joy and sorrow, hope and fear. They had come so far, but as they held each other beneath the moonlit sky, they both knew that their journey was only beginning.

When the time came for Mahi to leave again, they shared a long, lingering kiss, a promise woven into the bittersweet farewell. They didn't know what the future held, but for now, they were together. And that, for the moment, was enough.

" The Weight of Separation...."

During their conversation, Mahi sensed Aarav's struggle. "Are you okay?" she asked. "I want you to be happy." Aarav, with a heavy heart, replied, "I just... I wish we weren't so far apart again." They both felt the weight of separation closing in on them, yet they tried to remain supportive.

As Mahi prepared for her new life in Dubai, every step felt bittersweet. She spent days shopping for her move, filling bags with the pieces of a future she'd dreamt of for so long. Yet, each purchase reminded her of everything she was leaving behind—her family, her friends, and most of all, Aarav.

She had resigned from her retail job, wanting to spend her final days in India close to the ones she loved. Lucknow, draped in the icy chill of January 2015, felt like a city frozen in time—each day with Aarav passing faster than the last, yet lingering in her heart like the warmth of a fading flame.

One evening, with a crisp wind biting at their cheeks, Aarav called Mahi to meet him at a cozy café they often visited. The soft glow of dimmed lights and the hum of quiet conversations created an intimate atmosphere, as if the world outside had melted away.

Aarav's heart raced as he waited for her, his hands wrapped around a steaming cup of coffee to steady his nerves. His mind was a whirlwind of emotions—joy for Mahi's success, pride for the path she had chosen, but also fear. Fear of losing her to the distance, of time slipping through his fingers like the cold January air.

When Mahi walked in, her smile warmed the room, a lightness in her step despite the chill outside.

She sat across from him, eyes sparkling with anticipation, but there was also an unspoken understanding between them. They both knew this conversation was more than just about the future. It was about the love they had shared, the bond they were about to test once again.

Aarav took a deep breath, the words he had rehearsed a thousand times suddenly elusive. Finally, he reached across the table, his fingers brushing against hers. "Mahi, I know we've talked about this before, but with you leaving soon... I can't wait any longer."

Mahi's eyes softened, her heart skipping a beat as she felt the weight of what was coming. Aarav's voice, though steady, held a quiet vulnerability.

"I don't want to lose you, Mahi," he continued, his words raw, filled with emotion. "I know we've both committed to our dreams, but I love you. I want us to be together, no matter where life takes us."

Mahi's breath caught as Aarav reached into his pocket, pulling out a delicate ring—a simple, elegant band that shimmered like their shared hopes. He looked into her eyes, his gaze full of both love and uncertainty.

"Will you marry me?" he asked softly, his voice barely above a whisper, but in that moment, it was the only sound that mattered.

Tears welled up in Mahi's eyes as she smiled, her heart swelling with love for the man sitting before her. "Yes, Aarav," she whispered, her voice trembling with emotion. "Yes, I will."

They sat there, holding each other's gaze, the weight of the moment sinking in. But before they could even revel in their newfound commitment, reality crept back in. Mahi spoke, her voice steady despite the storm of emotions swirling inside her.

"You should resign from your job," she said, her fingers still entwined with his. "Focus on your UPSC. I'll go to Dubai and work for a year, but after that... we'll decide together. If you succeed, we'll stay in India. If not, you'll come to Dubai, and we'll build our life there. And next year, let's make it official with a formal engagement. That way, no matter where we are, we'll be one step closer to being together."

Aarav listened to her plan; his heart full of love but tinged with lingering doubt. Could they really make it work? Could they endure the distance again? Yet, as he looked into Mahi's eyes, he saw the same determination that had carried them through every challenge before. She believed in him, in them.

"We'll make this work," Mahi said firmly, squeezing his hand. Her confidence was unshakable, even as uncertainty hovered around them.

Aarav nodded, though the doubt still clung to the corners of his mind. But for now, they had each other. For now, they had this promise.

The next morning, they met again, their time together fleeting but precious. They wandered through the crowded streets of Lucknow, doing last-minute shopping for Mahi's move, their hands occasionally brushing as they walked side by side. Later, they shared a quiet lunch, savoring the simplicity of the moment—a brief pause in the whirlwind of change that awaited them.

As they parted that day, the weight of their new reality settled in, but there was also hope. In the cold, crisp air of that January day, Aarav and Mahi held on to the promise they had made—a promise to keep their love alive, no matter where the world took them.

Reflecting on Their Journey

Time seemed to slip through their fingers, like grains of sand scattering in the wind. February had arrived all too quickly, and with it, the reality of Mahi's departure. Her flight to Dubai was booked for the 23rd, and Aarav couldn't shake the gnawing feeling that their time together was running out.

On the night of the 22nd, they decided to have dinner at their favorite restaurant in Lucknow. The city was bathed in the soft glow of streetlights, and the air was filled with a quiet stillness that mirrored their emotions. They spent the evening reminiscing, laughing, and making plans for a future that felt so far away yet so vividly real in their hearts.

After dinner, they returned to Aarav's flat, the air between them thick with unspoken emotions. Mahi stayed the night, their last night together before her journey to Dubai. As they sat on the chairs, enveloped in the warmth of each other's presence, time seemed to slow down, yet it slipped away faster than they could grasp.

That night, they held each other closer than ever before. Mahi rested her head on Aarav's chest, listening to the rhythm of his heartbeat as he softly stroked her hair. They spoke of dreams, of the life they wanted to build, of how they would conquer the distance once again. They made plans—plans for the year apart, for their engagement, for a future where they would no longer have to say goodbye. Every word felt like a promise, whispered in the quiet intimacy of the night.

But beneath Aarav's calm demeanor was a silent struggle, a sinking realization he couldn't escape. Is this the last time? he wondered, his heart aching with the thought. His fingers gently traced the lines of her face, memorizing the feel of her skin, the curve of her smile, the softness of her hair. He kissed her, deeply, as if trying to imprint every part of her into his soul. But no matter how hard he held on, the night slipped away, passing in what felt like seconds.

And just like that, morning came.

Monday arrived with an unbearable heaviness. The sun rose, casting a pale light on the inevitability of their parting. Mahi's suitcase stood by the door, a stark reminder that this wasn't a dream—it was real. She was leaving.

Aarav, Mahi, and her family made their way to the airport in silence, the hum of the car engine the only sound. At the airport, they lingered at the departure gate, prolonging the inevitable goodbye. Aarav held Mahi's hand, his grip firm yet tender, as if letting go would mean losing her entirely.

Mahi looked at him, her eyes shimmering with both strength and sadness. "Things won't change," she said softly, her voice steady but filled with emotion. "No matter the distance, Aarav. We'll make this work."

Her words were meant to reassure him, but Aarav could feel the ache building in his chest, the fear of the unknown creeping in. He wanted to believe her, and deep down, he did. But the weight of their separation, the miles that would soon stretch between them, made it hard to breathe.

With a heavy heart, Mahi hugged her family and turned to Aarav one last time. She leaned in, her lips brushing his ear as she whispered, "I love you." Her breath was warm against his skin, and Aarav closed his eyes, holding onto the moment as if it were the last breath he'd ever take.

"I love you too, Mahi," he whispered back, his voice breaking.

And then, just like that, she was gone. Mahi walked away, her figure growing smaller as she headed towards the boarding gate. Aarav watched her, his eyes following every step until she disappeared into the crowd. His heart was a tangled mess of emotions—pride for the woman she had become, sorrow for the distance that now lay between them, and an overwhelming love that felt both endless and fragile.

As Mahi boarded the flight to Dubai, Aarav stood by the glass windows of the airport, watching the plane disappear into the sky. A part of him wanted to chase after her, to hold her one last time, to tell her that everything would be okay. But he knew that love, sometimes, meant letting go.

His chest tightened as he realized that this moment, this departure, wasn't just a temporary goodbye—it was the beginning of a new chapter. One where their love would be tested by time, by distance, by dreams. But even as the ache of separation weighed heavily on him, Aarav knew that Mahi was right. Distance couldn't change what they had.

It was a love built on trust, on shared dreams, on moments like this—where goodbyes were simply a promise that they would meet again.

Conclusion: A New Beginning......

Aarav standing at the airport, reflecting on their journey together. He acknowledges the pain of separation but also recognizes the strength it has given them both. As Mahi embarks on her new adventure, Aarav vows to pursue his UPSC dream, holding onto the promise they made to support one another.

Their story is far from over; it's merely transitioning into a new phase, where both must navigate their individual paths while cherishing the bond they share. The bittersweet essence of their love story lingers, leaving readers with a sense of hope and anticipation for what lies ahead.

The scene opens at the airport, with the protagonist standing there, staring at the bustling crowd but seeing nothing. His heart feels heavy, like lead in his chest. He watches the planes take off, each one carrying away something he can never reclaim. And then he realizes that one of them holds Mahi—the woman he thought he knew so well, the woman he had loved for four long years. But as she left without saying goodbye, he feels he never really knew her at all.

Reflection on the Beginning

He reflects on how it all started, remembering the first time they met. She was vibrant, full of life, and so different from anyone he had ever known. He was the small-town boy, in awe of her confidence, drawn to her like a moth to a flame. Her city-bred attitude was alien to him, but it fascinated him. He chuckles bitterly at the thought now—it was those very differences that he had come to adore that eventually became the cracks in their foundation.

Back then, he never thought the silence between them would stretch for this long. He remembers the awkward conversations, the misunderstandings, the small moments of joy when it seemed like they had found common ground. He used to wonder if love was supposed to feel this complicated, but he convinced himself it was just how their love was—a mix of unspoken promises and emotional distance.

The Struggle to Communicate

Aarav stood at his window, the soft hum of the city beneath him as silent tears burned his eyes. His phone lay on the table, still, lifeless, waiting for a message that he knew might never come. He had been tracking Mahi's flight obsessively, watching it inch closer to

Dubai, praying for her safety, but also for reassurance—some sign that everything between them was still okay. That their love could survive one more stretch of distance.

When her flight finally landed, his heart raced, and he dialled her new Dubai number immediately. The ringing was met with nothing but cold silence. Panic crept in, tightening his chest. He called again, then again—still unreachable. He stared at the screen, waiting for it to light up, waiting for her to tell him she had arrived safely.

Minutes felt like hours until his phone finally buzzed. It was Mahi.

"I have arrived safely at my hostel. No need to worry. We'll talk in the evening."

Her message was brief, almost mechanical, and it left Aarav unsettled. Still, he tried to brush it off—she was likely just tired. His mind grasped at excuses, refusing to acknowledge the growing pit in his stomach. The day stretched on, agonizingly slow, as Aarav waited for the evening to arrive. He sent her a message around 9:30 PM, eager to hear her voice, to see her face on Skype. But his WhatsApp message didn't deliver. Her profile picture had disappeared.

His heart skipped a beat. Something was wrong.

He called her number again. Nothing. Again and again, he tried, each unanswered ring feeding his growing anxiety. He waited through the night, staring at his phone in the dark, willing it to light up with her name. But it never did.

The next morning, desperate and confused, Aarav sent her an email. He kept it simple, trying not to sound panicked. *Your number is unreachable, and my WhatsApp messages aren't delivering. Is everything okay?*

Hours passed in excruciating silence before his inbox pinged. His hands shook as he opened her reply.

"Aarav, now it's over. I don't want to keep any more relations with you."

The words hit him like a punch to the gut. He read them over and over, unable to comprehend how Mahi—his Mahi—could have written something so cold, so final. His mind refused to accept it. How could she end everything with a single line? How could the girl who promised him the world, who vowed to make their love work, suddenly vanish like this?

His heart shattered, each beat a dull throb of disbelief and pain. Aarav spent the next few days in a haze, sending emails, calling every number he had for her, but it was useless. She had blocked him on every platform, shutting him out completely, leaving him alone with only his confusion and heartbreak.

Aarav wandered through the streets in a daze, feeling the walls of his heart close in. Lucknow, the city that once held their love, was now a graveyard of memories. The places they had shared together became cruel reminders of the future that had crumbled before him. Each day, the weight of her absence grew heavier, pressing down on his chest until he could barely breathe.

Each restaurant they had visited together, every street they had walked down hand-in-hand, became a reminder of her absence. The air in Lucknow felt suffocating, thick with memories that once brought him joy but now suffused his world with unbearable grief. He couldn't escape her. Every corner of the city echoed with her laughter, every gust of wind carried her scent, and every quiet moment was filled with the silence she had left behind.

He knew he couldn't stay any longer.

On May 23rd, 2015, Aarav packed a bag and left the city that had once been his home. It was no longer the Lucknow he had known; without Mahi, it felt foreign, empty. He couldn't bear it anymore. As he boarded the train, he typed out one final email to her, his last attempt to make sense of what had happened.

"I'm leaving Lucknow today. I stayed here because of you, but now you're not here anymore. I can't live here without you. I've decided to let go of my dream of becoming an IAS officer too. It all feels meaningless now."

His heart ached as he hit send, waiting, hoping—though he didn't know for what. Maybe for her to tell him she had made a mistake, that she missed him, that they could still fix this.

Hours later, a notification pinged. Mahi had replied.

"Ohk, that's great. Best wishes for your future."

The words were like a dagger to his heart. Simple, emotionless. The woman who had once filled his life with love, who had been his greatest support, was now a stranger. Her reply, so cold and detached, broke something deep inside him that he hadn't even realized was still intact.

Aarav sat there, staring at the screen, feeling the last remnants of hope slip through his fingers. Her response was the final nail in the coffin of their love. He had lost her—completely, irrevocably.

In that moment, Aarav realized that sometimes, love doesn't end in a grand, dramatic fashion. Sometimes, it ends in silence, in an unanswered call, in a text message that never gets delivered. And sometimes, the person who was once your everything can vanish with a few indifferent words, leaving you to pick up the shattered pieces of a life you no longer recognize.

And just like that, Mahi was gone—not only from his life, but from the very fabric of his existence. And all that was left for Aarav was the echo of a love that had slipped away, leaving him in the ruins of what could have been.

Four Years of Love and Loneliness

The years had passed quickly, with life moving forward, but it was like they had stopped moving together. The once-promising future they had discussed—dreaming of travel, success, and shared happiness—had quietly dissolved into something neither of them could recognize anymore. He remembers the late nights, lying in bed next to her, but feeling miles apart. It wasn't that they fought; it was that they had simply drifted away from each other, a slow, quiet unravelling.

He wonders when it started to change—when they began building walls instead of bridges. Perhaps it was during the arguments they never fully resolved, or the times they chose silence over confrontation. Or maybe it was when they stopped dreaming together and began living separate lives, even when they were in the same room.

Mahi's Departure: A Heartbreak Without Words

The image of her at the airport haunts him. She stood there, looking at him with eyes that once sparked with affection, now empty and distant. She didn't have to say anything—her silence said it all. No explanation, no goodbye, just a quiet departure. A lump forms in his throat as he replays the moment over and over in his mind. He wanted to reach out, to ask why, to beg her to stay, but he couldn't. Something inside him knew that this was how it had to end.

Her leaving like that, without a word, feels cruel, but at the same time, he knows it wasn't out of malice. It was just who Mahi was—she wasn't the kind of person who could break hearts with words. She did it with actions, or in this case, inaction. In the end, it was perhaps her way of protecting herself, and maybe even him.

Grief and Acceptance

The grief comes in waves—some moments it feels unbearable, like he's drowning in memories of her, and in others, there's a hollow emptiness that consumes him. He feels the loss not just of Mahi, but of the person he was with her, and the future he thought they would have.

There's an overwhelming urge to call her, to ask why she left without a word. But he knows that even if she answered, the closure he's seeking would never come from her. It would have to come from within. He starts to realize that sometimes love doesn't end with the slamming of a door, but with a quiet, gradual departure. Mahi's silence had always been there—it was just that, until now, he hadn't been ready to face it.

Growth and Letting Go

As painful as it is, he understands that this chapter of his life is over. He stands there, lost in the crowd at the airport, knowing that when he walks out of those doors, he'll have to start his life again—alone, but stronger. He realizes that love, no matter how deep, sometimes isn't enough to keep two people together. And that's okay. Their time together had taught him so much—about love, vulnerability, and the importance of communication.

He takes one last deep breath, trying to hold on to the last pieces of her. Then, with each step toward the exit, he lets them go. He lets her go. It's not the ending he wanted, but it's the one he has, and he'll learn to live with it.

Moving Forward

The streets outside the airport are as busy as ever, but something inside him has changed. He's not the same boy who left his small town with dreams in his heart. The city, Mahi, and the heartbreak have shaped him into someone new. Someone who understands that not every love story has a happy ending, but every ending carries the seeds of a new beginning.

As he walks away, he silently thanks Mahi—not for the love they shared, but for the lessons she taught him in her leaving. For teaching him that sometimes the most painful goodbyes are the ones left unsaid, and that silence can be the loudest sound in the world.

After four years of shared memories, growth, and silent battles, the relationship that once thrived on unspoken emotions and contrasting worlds reached its inevitable breaking point. Mahi's departure at the Dubai airport, without a word or farewell, was a stark and sudden end to what had been a tumultuous yet profound connection. It wasn't just the distance or their differences that tore them apart—it was the weight of unsaid things, the fear of vulnerability, and the unspoken boundaries they never fully broke.

For the protagonist, the silence was more deafening than any confrontation. Mahi's decision to leave without explanation left him grappling with unanswered questions and the realization that some chapters in life remain unfinished, no matter how much you try to rewrite them. In the end, it wasn't the clash of their worlds that ended their relationship, but the emotional distance that had slowly crept in.

In that moment of watching Mahi fade into the distance, Aarav knew that their chapter had closed in a way that neither of them expected. It was not a grand goodbye, nor a dramatic ending; it was the quiet, piercing reality that not all love stories end in resolution. The silence between them was more telling than words could have been, marking the end of their shared dreams and the beginning of separate paths.

Aarav, now left to confront life without Mahi, embarked on a journey of self-discovery—one that would change him profoundly. While Mahi carved out a new life of her own, perhaps with the same drive and ambition that once drew him to her, Aarav had to learn how to live with the void she left behind. Their separation was not just the end of their love, but the start of something new for both of them.

The story doesn't end here. ***What happens next—how Aarav rebuilds, and what Mahi's choices mean for her future—will unravel in the second part of this book***. Their lives, though separated, remain intertwined in ways neither of them fully understands yet. And while they walk different paths now, their journey might not be as over as it seems.

www.ingramcontent.com/pod-product-compliance
Lightning Source LLC
LaVergne TN
LVHW041944070526
838199LV00051BA/2901